TUFF INK PUBLICATIONS PRESENTS

Bad Blood

a novel by

Tuffy

Black and Nobel Books
Retail & Wholesale
215-965-1559
1409 W. Erie Ave
Philadelphia, PA 19140
Email: Blacknoble1@yahoo.com
Mon - Sat 7am - 7pm
www.weshiptoprisons.com

The accounts of this book are fiction and in no way represent any person or event.

Introduction Copyright © 2009 by
Tuff Ink Publication
P.O. Box 24540
Philadelphia, Pa 19120

Library of Congress Control Number: 2010921601
ISBN# 978-0-9844285-0-2
Cover Design: www.StricklyGraphics.com
Editor: Ann Marie Escher

Printed in the United States of America

Dedication

First and foremost, I would like to thank Allah for giving me another avenue to hustle. The contents of this book do not represent our beliefs but please continue to work on me as a person and as a believer. Ameen.

This book is dedicated to West Philly's own Macky Woods Pratt, Tyree Zealous Torrence, and Braheem "Bra Strap" Smalls. Damn, y'all cut me deep when Allah called you back. I love y'all right now the same as I did when y'all were here. I still love what y'all loved and hate what y'all hated.

Acknowledgments

I have to thank all of the people who believed in and supported me when everybody else counted me out. Thanks to all of the people who still pressed #5 when I called from the jail. Furthermore, I would like to thank my Mother Gwen and my Aunt Ellen for holding me down all of my life. Y'all are jewels but y'all got it from Grandmom. Even on her death bed, she held this whole family down...Thank You, Lady Dee.

To my children, please know that y'all are my world and, as always, y'all can turn to Daddy for any and everything. To the four other Torrence boys, with whom I was raised, Sput, Barry, Ducky, and Marty, I love y'all and we are one and the same. My success is y'alls success. I'll hold y'all down as I always did. Wuda, you are more like a son to me than a little cousin. The Torrence family is very large but I want to say that I love you all and the tight bond that we share. To my other blood line, the Veneys, I love you all as well. We lost my Dad and Cousin Sharon while I was down and I miss them both dearly.

Now to the homies....this may take awhile. Ha-Ha. To the owners of Cash is King Publishing, Shaahir and B-Easy, I love y'all, dudes, and I wish you two much success! You guys are good dudes and like family to me. Shaahir, thanks for showing me so much game. CEO in stores now. To my proven best friend, Ronald Austin, we've held each other down since childhood. You've been a life-long blessing, I love you, dawg. Damn, the best thing that came out of this situation was meeting my little brother Omar "Jim-Jim" Miller. By the time this book hits the streets, we'll be pulling them Bentleys back out. I still got the money machines my nigga. Now that we're linked, the niggas are mad and the chicks are confused. To Shawn "Shiz" Williams, you're my nigga to the end and you've proven that. I got you, my nigga. To Marshay, damn, my nigga…you are my family and you're still the realest nigga in this watered-down-ass system. I haven't turned my back on you and I won't. Herb, I love you, homie, and I'm anticipating your book. You know I ride for and with you. A big shout-out goes to Qaseemah. Without you, there would be no Tuff Ink Publications. You've been a blessing and this entire company is the fruit of your labor. Thank You! Jig "Manny" you know what it is, Cousin. You're my boy by far. I love you. Thelma, you are the best cousin that I could ever ask for. You've been with me forever and you've always made it clear to everybody that your cousin is the best that ever done it. I love you, girl. Nina and the entire Moss family, thanks for always having my back, I love y'all. Sending love to my sisters, Indira, Mandy, and Sabrina. Shakour and Sharif, y'all are my family and a perfect example of strength. Even with facing over 20 years, y'all have managed to hold down your people on the streets. When shit ain't right, y'all make an OG call and get things right. I always tell Sonya that niggas don't deserve folks like y'all. Zakiyah and Paiger, y'all are my folks, too. Y'all know what it is and I love y'all. To my little brothers, Brad and Cal, Tim, Nino (Take Down Records), and the whole C.P. (Capital Punishment), I love y'all niggas. I'm C.P. forever.

Shout-outs to Bub "The Warden" White, Big Lou, Cag, Frost, O-Ski, Rome, Moncho, Megget, Erick, Derrick, Tidy, Eggy, Space, Smells, Lemeo, Ivan, Rell

(R.I.P.), Boo, Baby Calvin, Woody, Curt, Littles, Baby Dee, Ockie, Wayne Cherry, Boo Cherry (R.I.P.), Juice, Twizzy, Antman (R.I.P.), Dana (R.I.P.), Miles (R.I.P.), Frank (39th Street), Sam, Donuts (R.I.P.), Devince, Ish, Omillio, Sparks, Lo Ball (B-More), Cam (38th Street), Kenny, and Omega (Vineland). South Philly Little Clark, Butter Felton, Nate, North Philly Tow Truck Joe, my little brother, Reem (Richard Allen), Ceasar (Norris St), Malik & Naim (23rd Street), Ty (Norris St), West Philly Chanel (Ms CeeCee), Nine, Calvin, Little Man, Marcel, Lez, the Meesle, Marv, Spence, EA (Back to Basic), Spade (MF), Lill, Butter, Boo, Ty, John, Stoney, Joey B., Azeem (CB Dub) Gees (Pottstown). Delaware, Mustafa (Level 5) Shawn Gee$, Black (Shannon), Sidiq (Donny), and Dawud. Shy (Master Street), Boop, Will and Nafee (Frankford), Baby Boy (Belvin), Booburg (R.I.P.). My Camden niggas, K-Reem (Tuff Ink's V.P.), Shakour, 45 Trev, Beans, Skeet & Mall, and Cam.

To all the Philly Authors, Terri Woods, Tenia Jamilla, Golden Girl, Nikki Hawkins, Shawn Pettiway, Jimmy Da Saint, Mustafa, and Amir, just to name a few, keep y'alls pens moving so Philly can keep it's stamp on the game. Shout-out to all the Urban Writers in every hood.

Last, but not least, to all the readers that support the game…thanks for your support. Tuff Ink will always give y'all quality books to enjoy. For our readers that are in jail, I hope that our books will help your time go a little smoother and allow you all to see that there are other avenues to get paper. Stay Up.

Prologue

Ern pulled up to his house in his work truck. He sat in the car thinking of the conversation he had with his right-hand-man, Tone. He had expressed to Tone that he was done with breaking his kilos down and selling them in portions. Tone understood where Ern was coming from because they were getting too many kilos and far too much money to be breaking down at this point. What Tone didn't understand was the fact that Ern was prepared to leave the streets alone all together at the end of the year. Ern had made enough money and he had a multitude of legit ventures that would allow him to live comfortably. His focus now was on spending time with his wife and watching his son grow up.

Tone didn't understand how niggas always talked about retiring from the streets. He didn't have a wife or kids, so he was married to and his commitment was to the streets. As far as he was concerned, Ern could retire right now because he was prepared to be a bricklayer until death do him part. As Ern put the key in the door, he was thinking of how ignorant Tone was. He had to smile at the thought of Tone acting dramatic and saying over and over with a silly smirk on his face, "I'm married to the game and I don't believe in divorce."

Ern genuinely loved Tone and he would never try to belittle him by telling him how dumb he appeared by considering the game to be his wife. Ern knew that the game didn't love nobody. His train of thought was broken when he opened the door to his house and his son ran up to meet him.

Micky was getting bigger by the day and the older he got the more he resembled Ern. He was Ern's only child and his pride and joy.

"Dad, the Lakers play the Sixers this weekend at the Wachovia Center. Please tell me that we have tickets."

"We always have tickets."

"Yeeeesssss!"

Micky was excited about going to the game. He took the bags out of Ern's hand and put them in the kitchen before he ran upstairs to take his shower before going to bed. Ern walked into the kitchen where he was greeted with a hug and a kiss from Sharon. She had his dinner plate on the table already warmed up. They sat at the table together and discussed each other's day as Ern ate his dinner.

Once he finished eating, Ern went upstairs to his office to straighten out a few things while Sharon cleaned the kitchen. His office was his own space, he would often go there to clear his mind and obtain tranquility. He sat behind his desk listening to his voicemail on the intercom of his business line. He picked up the picture that sat on his desk of him, Tone, Bingo, and Champ. They were all childhood friends but he looked at them more as brothers. As far as Ern was concerned, it was a family photo. The picture was taken at A.I.'s All Star Weekend Party in the Gallery. He smiled at the picture as he reminisced on how they outshined all the out-of-towners that came into Philly for that weekend. The ringing of his phone forced him to cut his flashback short.

"Yizzo."

"Yizzo, my nigga. I'm just making sure you got in the crib safe," Tone said, checking in on Ern.

"Yeah, I'm good."

"Ok Ern, I'll see you tomorrow."

They said their good-byes and hung up. Ern finished up in his office and went into his bedroom where Sharon was already waiting. She had finished in the kitchen ten minutes ago. Micky peeked his head in their room to say goodnight before he got into bed. Sharon and Ern talked briefly before they dozed off with the TV on.

Micky's screams filled the air and woke Ern and Sharon from their sleep. Before they could fully understand what was going on, they were looking down the barrels of guns held by three masked men standing beside their bed. Ern had never felt so helpless in his life. Losing his life came with the game, he knew that without a doubt, but he never planned on risking the life of his wife and son.

"Whatever y'all want I'll give it to y'all...just don't hurt my family," Ern pleaded.

"Shut the fuck up. If you follow instructions your family will be okay," yelled the masked man, who seemed to be in charge.

Just then, Micky came running into the room with nothing but his drawers on. He somehow managed to break free from the men who were in his room. He ran up to his dad and hugged him.

"One more dumb-ass move like that and somebody is going to get shot," the same man confirmed, while looking at Ern.

"I have plenty of money but there is only chump change here. I'll pay y'all whatever, just let me and my family go."

"Ern, I know you're a wealthy man. We've been instructed not to hurt your family so be easy. I do need you to tell your son and your wife to go with my men and for them to follow what's asked of them."

Ern felt like shit having to send his wife and son off to follow the commands of a bunch of thugs but he knew it was their best chance at surviving. Sharon followed behind the masked men in her bra and boy shorts. She held Micky's hand tightly as he attempted to look back to see his Dad. They got to the end of the hallway and the men instructed them to lie down so they could duct-tape their hands and feet. They took care of Sharon first. When they were about to restrain Micky, several shots rang out from the room Ern was in. Micky yanked away and ran toward the room. Before he got to the door, the masked men came running out and headed down the steps. Micky ran to his father's side but it was too late. His hero was dead and his world was crushed...

Chapter 1

Sharon sat in her car with tears in her eyes. She had become immune to the rumors about the death of her husband, Ern. It had been five years since Ern was killed in front of Sharon and their 13-year-old son, Micky. Sharon had heard various rumors in the past concerning Ern's murder. Some said it was because he owed money to the Columbians. Others said he was killed because he crossed niggas in the streets for a connect. The biggest rumor of them all was that Ern was killed because it was discovered he was an informant. Sharon learned to cope with all that however, what she heard today blew her mind.

She was in the salon getting her hair done when her hair stylist, Meeka, told her what was currently being said on the streets about Ern's murder. She told Sharon that she heard Sharon and Tone set Ern up to be killed so they could run off with his money. Although that was a believable scenario, it was not the truth. Anyone who knew Sharon knew she loved Ern with all her heart and she would never cross him for any amount money. The only thing that made the rumor seem to have truth to it was the fact that, a year after Ern died, Sharon moved in with Tone.

Tone was Ern's homie and business partner. They grew up together and came up in the streets together.

They started off nickel-and-diming in the streets of Philly just like any other hustler who starts out in the coke game. Within a year's time, Ern and Tone were running the streets. They were both from West Philly, but conducted their business all around the city. They had a connect in Houston which contributed to their being ahead of the average players in Philly. Because they were able to get their coke cheaper than the average player, they were able to sell their coke cheaper and, because of that, they had a lot of clientele.

Tone and Ern were like day and night. Everybody liked Ern because he was mild-mannered and he looked out for them. Tone, on the other hand, was arrogant and selfish. When news of Ern's death hit the streets a lot of people were hurt, and a lot of the players wished that it was Tone who was killed instead of Ern. When news that Sharon was living with Tone hit the streets the following year it looked suspicious to some people, although others looked at it as a friend being supportive of his dead homie's wife and son.

As time went by, it became obvious to everyone that Sharon and Tone were together. It gave many people a bad taste in their mouths to know Tone was fucking Ern's wife, but they would never speak about it around Tone or anybody that would tell him. They knew Tone would either cut their food supply or their throat. Now that Sharon heard this rumor, she began to wonder how she fell in love with Ern's friend. She thought to herself, *Out of all the niggas in Philly, why Tone?*

When she initially moved in with Tone, it was innocent. She was depressed for the whole year following Ern's death. Tone always checked on her, although Ern left her more than enough money to take care of her and

6

their son. Tone would still come around to give her money and help with the maintenance of the properties Ern left her. Tone looked after Micky from day one as if he were his own son. When Sharon had a nervous breakdown during the one-year anniversary of Ern's death, Micky stayed with Tone. When Sharon got out of the hospital, Tone convinced her to stay with him until she was back on her feet and feeling well enough to go home. Sharon moved in with Tone and had been living with him ever since.

Tone never made her feel uncomfortable. When Micky stayed with his Aunt Deb for the weekend for his birthday, Sharon was left alone with Tone. Tone convinced Sharon to go out and have a drink with him. They had such a good time that Sharon felt alive again for the first time in a long time. She was so tipsy when they got back to the house that she turned the music up in the living room and began dancing all up on Tone. The night got out of control, but they were both enjoying themselves. Tone ended up fucking Sharon and, to her surprise, he was a better lover than she ever had before. From that day on, they were a couple. Sharon never gave their relationship a second thought until today. She started her car and drove toward the house she shared with Tone in Dover, Delaware.

Sharon often talked to herself and questioned her own judgment. She re-evaluated her situation by saying to herself, *Tone is a great lover. He looks out for Micky and he was there for me when I needed someone most. This shit is trifling and it's a slap in the face to Ern. Damn, how did I get stuck like this? I really love Tone, but I don't know what to do.* While she was deep in her thoughts, she heard the phone ring.

"Hello," Sharon said, putting the phone to her ear and turning the music down.

"What's up, Sharon? This is Wanna."

"Bitch, I know who it is. That's why I pay for caller ID." They both laughed.

"What are we doing tonight, Sharon?"

"You know, it's whatever with me."

"Well...my future husband is having an invitation-only party and I've got an invitation for you."

"You still on Champ's head, huh?" Sharon asked, with a hint of sarcasm. "

"Hell yeah, he be talking that brother-and-sister shit but I'll get him where I want him in due time," Sharon laughed.

"Bitch, you are a borderline stalker."

Wanna ignored Sharon's comment and continued with what she was saying.

"He's been my personal project for years, and through all that play brother-and-sister shit I've gotten to know him, and he's all the man that I need."

"Well...I'll tell Tone that I'm going with you and I'll call you back."

They hung up and Sharon called Tone who picked up on the second ring.

"Hello."

"What's up, Pretty Tone?" That was Sharon's name for Tone and he loved to hear her say it, especially when they were around people.

"What's up, baby-girl?"

"Nothing. I was just letting you know that Wanna has invitations to her play-brother Champ's invite-only party and she wants me to go with her."

"Go ahead, I ain't trippin'. You know Champ is my man."

"You know I have to check with you, daddy."

"That's why you're my baby-girl."

As soon as they hung up, Sharon called Wanna back.

"Hello," Wanna said.

"What time are we out?" asked Sharon.

"We'll hook up about ten."

"Oh yeah, before we hang up, Tone told me to tell you to stop stalking Champ."

"Tell Tone that somebody's got to do it."

They both shared another laugh before they hung up.

As Sharon arrived home she began to realize just how blessed she is. The home she shared with Tone had four bedrooms, two-and-a-half bathrooms, and a four-car garage. Micky was now 18 and living alone, so it was just Tone, Sharon, and their teacup yorkie, Cavalli. Sharon had decorated the house: she loved earth tones so they were evident throughout the home's decor. Her kitchen had brick-front walls with stainless steal appliances and marble tiles imported from Italy. Tone added a flat-screen TV behind the island wall so Sharon could be entertained while she cooked. Although she loved the entire home, the kitchen took her breath away. It was the kitchen she always dreamed of, and Tone spared no expense to give it to her. The entire house was a site to see, it looked like something out of an interior design magazine.

Sharon walked through the house and immediately let Cavalli out into the backyard. Although she was house-trained to go on pads, Cavalli didn't use them. She was excited to see Sharon who, being home far more often than Tone, let her out back to do her business and run and play. After she let Cavalli back into the house, Sharon went upstairs and ran some hot water in her kidney-shaped Jacuzzi. She went to check her voicemail as she waited for the tub to fill.

Once she returned to the bathroom, she slid down into the tub and replayed the whole conversation she had with Meeka about Ern. She began to realize that it wasn't much of a conversation. It was more like Meeka was gossiping and trying to pick her for info.

I've got to watch that newsy bitch. She probably made up that rumor herself. Besides, Wanna told me to watch that hatin' bitch. I'm finding a new hair dresser, she thought.

Sharon felt eased by her decision. She folded her warm cloth and draped it over her eyes as she laid back to enjoy her bath.

Wanna and Sharon arrived at the party around 11:30. As expected, Champ was doing it big. All the ballers had their big cars out tonight, and the who's who of the city were there. Champ was that nigga in the city that the players loved and the haters respected. The party was held at the African American Museum on Seventh and Arch Streets in Center City. It was hosted by Shamara, a local radio personality. It was a classy party. No sneakers, jeans, or white tee shirts. It was open-bar and there was free seafood all night. Champ was a street nigga but he had corporate class. There were a lot of street niggas at his party, but there were also a host of basketball players, boxers, and white collar workers present as well.

As Wanna and Sharon walked up to their table in the VIP section, they noticed two bottles of Rosé waiting for them. When Champ walked up, he greeted them with a hug and a quick kiss on the cheek; first Sharon, then Wanna who held on a little longer.

"You going to make me forget you're my sister," Champ whispered in Wanna's ear.

"Nigga, I love you, but I'm not your sister," Wanna remarked, in a seductive yet assertive tone.

"Damn...that's cold," Champ said, as he pulled back from Wanna to look her in the face.

Wanna smiled and replied, "No...that's real."

"I'll keep that in mind," Champ remarked, as he stepped back, looking Wanna up and down.

Wanna was killing a Rachel Roy, one-of-a-kind skirt with some Christian Louboutin heels. Wanna's mother-of-pearl-faced Rolex dangled on her arm and gave her light brown skin an extra glow. She had a tight body that was sick. Champ was distracted from staring at his so-called sister's ass by the sound of Sharon's voice.

"Thanks for the Rosé," Sharon said.

"I didn't buy the bottles, he did," Champ said, pointing at Tone who was walking toward them. When he reached them, he shook Champ's hand and gave Wanna a hug and a peck on the cheek before her turned to kiss Sharon.

"You didn't tell me you were coming," she said.

"I know...because I wasn't going to come, but when you said you were coming I had to come see my boo," Tone said, with a smile on his face.

While Tone and Sharon talked, Wanna and Champ walked off. Wanna went to the restroom and Champ went to talk to Micky who was at the bar with two chicks. Micky was Champ's heart since he was a baby. Although Champ never spoke on the death of Ern, or Tone and Sharon's relationship, the whole situation cut him deep. He was cool with both Tone and Ern since childhood so he never offered his opinion about the ugliness of Tone and Sharon's relationship. Instead, he just kept true to his friendship with Ern and always looked after Micky. To see Micky as a grown man out mingling at his party made Champ think of how fast Micky had grown and how much he reminded him of Ern.

Micky noticed Champ staring at him.

"What's up with you, Unc," Micky asked. He always looked at Champ as an uncle, even when his father was alive.

"Nothing, Nephew...I was just peeping your style and noticing that you're as smooth as your father," Champ said, shaking Micky's hand and looking at the chicks next to him. Micky noticed Champ giving the chicks the once-over, so he introduced them.

"Unc, this is Amanda and Keisha. Keisha and Amanda, this is my Uncle Champ," Micky said, palming Amanda's ass to let Champ know she was his.

"Nice to meet you ladies," Champ said, shaking the girls' hands.

The ladies responded at the same time with, "Nice to meet you, too."

Wanna walked up at the end of the introductions.

"What's up, Nephew," Wanna said, hugging Micky.

"Nothing, Aunt Wanna...I'm just chilling," Micky said, as the DJ put on Young Jeezy's *I Put On*.

"Come on, Champ, this is my song," Wanna said, as she pulled Champ by the arm and led him to the dance floor full of people.

They were enjoying themselves in the middle of the dance floor with everybody else but, now that Champ was really observing Wanna, it seemed as if his guests were a sea full of strangers. He felt like it was just him and Wanna out there on the floor. Wanna was grinding her fat ass all up on Champ's ten-and-a-half inch dick which was fully erect by the middle of the song and felt like 12 inches bulging through his Cavalli slacks.

"Damn, Champ...I thought you said no guns allowed," Wanna said, in a sexy tone with lust in her eyes.

"Who got a gun in here?" Champ said, breaking out of his lustful trance and missing her joke.

"You got that 12 gauge riot-pump on my ass, right where it belong," Wanna said, with a smile that exposed her dimple and white teeth. They shared a laugh and danced to three more songs caught up in their own world, with their own lust, own jokes, and own laughs.

"Damn, Wanna, you're not the little sister I used to know," said Champ.

"I've been trying to tell you that, Champ, but you weren't trying to hear that I'm a big girl in every way."

"Well I guess I got to see what you're like as my new girl," Champ said. He turned and winked at Wanna before he disappeared into the crowd.

Wanna stood there hoping he wasn't just talking. She knew so much about Champ. She knew he didn't talk just to be talking and she knew he hadn't had a girlfriend for the past two years. Before she could finish fantasizing, Sharon grabbed her by the arm.

"Damn, girl...you and Champ were glued together on the dance floor."

"Yeah, Sharon, and it was worth it. I loved it girl," Wanna said, with a devilish smile.

"Girl...Champ ain't paying you no mind so you better find one of those fine brothers floating around in here."

"That's where you're wrong, Sharon. I got him. He just said that the brother/sister stuff is out the window."

"We'll see," Sharon said, with her hands on her hips.

Wanna looked at her and said, "I got two words for you, Sharon."

"And what are they?" Sharon asked.

"Hi, hater!" The girls laughed.

They enjoyed the rest of the party, as did everyone else. While they were driving to Wanna's house to get Sharon's car, Wanna got a call from Champ. He told her that he would like to take her out tomorrow and she agreed. As soon as she hung up, she informed Sharon that she had an official date with Champ. As they pulled up to Wanna's house, Sharon jumped out and got into her car to go home. Wanna went inside to relish in the progress of her evening.

Chapter 2

Champ was up early. He knew he had a lot to do and wanted to get it out of the way so he could take Wanna out. He thought about her all night and all morning. He couldn't understand how he hadn't noticed how sexy and on-the-ball Wanna had grown to be. He vowed to make her his chick. After thinking of her, and how much she had going on, he realized that she would be a perfect fit in his world.

Damn, I hope that pussy is good, he thought as he pulled up to Champions, his breakfast store on Germantown Avenue. As he parked, he noticed that Ducky was already there waiting for him. Ducky was Ern's young bull. He used to put in work for Ern and Tone, but when Ern died he got so wild that Tone cut him off. Champ ended up taking Ducky under his wing and now he was his favorite young bull. Being with Champ helped Ducky put things in perspective and Champ noticed the Ducky only gets wild when it's called for. He had mad respect and genuine love for Champ because he treated him as good as Ern did when he was alive.

Ducky had serious thoughts of killing Tone. It was Champ's relationship with Tone and Ern's love for the nigga that kept Ducky from showing his contempt for Tone for cutting him off.

Champ walked up to Ducky, shook his hand and hugged him saying, "Damn Duck, you're always on time."

"Champ, Ern always said, 'never keep a good man waiting' and you're one of the best niggas I know," Ducky said, smiling and exposing his signature chipped tooth.

"Let's go inside and get something to eat," Champ said, leading the way into the breakfast store. Once inside, the new waitress stepped up to them not realizing that Champ was the owner.

"Hi, welcome to Champions where we serve all beef, turkey, and chicken products. My name is Rhonda and I'll be serving you gentlemen today," Rhonda said, leading them to a booth in the back.

Champ actually liked the way she was handling them as customers. Rhonda picked up on a weird vibe when people started whispering, waving, and pointing as she led them to their seats. While she was taking their order, Ms. Gail, the store manager, came over.

"Rhonda, I'll take care of these guys," she said.

Before Rhonda could say anything or walk away Champ cut in.

"No, Gail, she's doing a good job, and if you hired her you did a great job," he said.

"Okay, boss, but if you need me just call and I'll be right over," Gail said, acknowledging his status.

She looked directly at Rhonda to make certain she got the hint. Rhonda continued to take their order. When she got close enough to the cook, Nate, she passed him the order and whispered in his ear.

"Is that the owner?"

"Yeah, that's Champ, and he's the best employer I've had in 20 years of working in these greasy-spoon spots."

Rhonda had mistakenly thought the owner was an old dude with cheap suits who was out of touch with common people. She never suspected a 30-something, black man of Champ's caliber. She noticed his style. He was wearing Gucci sneakers with some PRPS jeans and shirt. He wasn't too flashy with the jewels either. In fact, he only wore one piece, a platinum Pearlmaster Rolex. Rhonda thought his style was very classy and, as a result, she vowed to stay away from stereotyping anyone from today on out. She sadly mistook her employer as a drug dealer, not that she had any problems with drug dealers. In fact, during her past three days of working at Champions, she realized that they were the best tippers. As she brought the food to the table she said, "Let me know if y'all need anything else."

"We're fine, thanks," Champ said, before Rhonda walked away.

Rhonda came back 20 minutes later to check on them and Champ asked for the bill. As Rhonda placed their check on the table, Champ laid a 50-dollar bill on top of it.

"I'll be right back with your change," said Rhonda, picking up the check.

"Don't worry about it," said Champ, as he and Ducky walked out.

Rhonda stood dazed at the sizable tip as she watched the two men leave the restaurant.

When he got outside, he exchanged cars with Ducky. Ducky took the Cadillac Escalade that Champ pulled up in and Champ took the Benz CL-63 that Ducky had been driving. Champ left 20 bricks of coke in the Cadillac for

Ducky. Ducky knew the rules. Champ never passed bags in the streets nor did he discuss business on the phone. Champ went about his business while Ducky headed to the detail shop to unload the bricks from the stash box of the Caddy.

~~~~~

Tone was upset about the amount of business he was losing. Rocky was one of Tone's best customers for the last few years. Normally, Rocky would cop about seven kilos a week off Tone, but now he claimed that business had been slow for the last couple of months, so he was only getting two at a time. Tone decided to put his ears to the street. He heard through the gossip that Rocky was still serving a lot of work. Since he knew that he was only selling Rocky a brick or two a week, he assumed Rocky was copping off somebody else. His hunch was that Rocky was getting his work from either Bingo or Champ.

Bingo came up with Tone, Ern, and Champ, but moved to South Philly when Ern got killed. Although he relocated, he still represented West Philly. He was still cool with Tone but they didn't do business. Word was that Bingo stumbled across a Miami connect and, as a result, had been flooding the city. Bingo didn't cut his coke, he gave it up how it came…raw. Champ's business did not stagger because he served his work raw as well and had a good connect.

Tone, on the other hand, had a good connect, but he was so greedy that he cut his coke. His customers feared him for one reason or another, so they would never say fuck him and buy off someone else. Instead, they just grabbed less work from Tone and got the bulk of it from Bingo. Tone was going to pay Bingo a visit, but first he wanted to see what Bam found out about Rocky. He was waiting on Bam, his favorite young bull, to see what he grabbed from Rocky. He sent Bam to get a brick from Rocky to see if it was his, Champ's, or Bingo's work. The doorbell rang. After looking through the peephole and seeing Bam, Tone let him in.

"What's up, little homie?" Tone said, as he shook Bam's hand.

"Nothing, I just had to sell that nigga a story about you cutting me off before he would even talk about selling me some work."

Tone was intrigued and asked, "Did he sell you something?"

Bam reached up under his shirt and pulled a brick from his waistband.

"Yeah...this," he replied.

To Tone's surprise, it was the same brick he had sold Rocky two days ago.

"This nigga is clever," Tone said, in a low voice while nodding his head.

"Why you say that?" asked Bam.

"How much did he charge you?" asked Tone in return.

"He took $19,000," Bam replied.

"I charged him $19,000, so how can he charge you the same thing and not make a dime?"

"Tone, I don't know, but that's what he charged me."

Tone was irritated.

"Bam, that nigga didn't buy your story that I cut you off so he gave you the work that I gave him just in case you brought it back to me."

Bam considered the situation and admitted to himself that Rocky was clever.

"Now what, Tone?"

"Nothing…we'll get to the bottom of it. We're going to holler at Bingo, and I'll ask him straight up if he's serving Rocky."

"I'm with whatever you're with, Tone," said Bam.

"Okay, Bam, put that brick under the couch and we'll go down to Bingo's tire shop."

They rode in Tone's CLS 55 Benz listening to Jadakiss' *Last Kiss* CD. When they pulled up, Tone noticed another one of his customers, little Tooky, pulling off.

"Damn, this nigga must be hitting all of my customers," Tone said, to himself although loud enough for Bam to hear.

"That was Tooky, wasn't it?" Bam questioned, although he was sure it was.

"Yeah, that was his bitch ass," Tone spat out as he got out of the car.

Bam followed Tone into the tire shop. Once inside, Tone noticed Bingo's brother, Teddy, and two of his homies watching basketball. Teddy never liked Tone and never tried to hide it. He noticed Tone when he walked in, but he kept watching the game.

"Yo, is Bingo here?" Tone asked.

Teddy didn't say a word; he just picked up the phone and began talking.

"Yo, B, do you want to see Tone?" he asked. As he hung up, he instructed his goon.

"Show dude to the back," he said, as he gestured his hand in a dismissive motion.

Tone followed the guy to the back, but instructed Bam to stay up front with Teddy. Bingo was sitting at his desk when Tone came in. After they exchanged greetings, Tone cut straight to the chase.

"Damn, Bingo, you know that Rocky and Tooky have been my customers for the longest."

Caught by surprise, Bingo stayed quiet for a minute. When he finally spoke up, Bingo said, "Yeah, and what that got to do with me?"

"I heard they've been buying off of you," Tone lied.

"I don't serve them niggas, I barely even know them," Bingo spat.

"Damn, I thought we were better homies than you lying to me about some nigga crossing me."

By this time, Bingo was upset and could not believe Tone's audacity.

"Look, Tone, I don't know them niggas. I don't owe you shit!" His voice became elevated. "You're really insulting me coming to my place of business about some small time niggas. Now, if you must know, them niggas are Teddy's people and I don't get into my little brother's affairs," he concluded.

Tone felt like a nut and he knew he couldn't say anything to Teddy because it would be a shootout on the spot. Tone also knew that he couldn't win at the tire shop because Teddy and his boys out-numbered him and Bam.

"My bad, Bingo, I'm out of pocket," Tone said, before he left the office. When he got back out front he nodded to Bam and they were out.

~~~~~

Champ finished his running around eight that evening. He went to pick up Wanna an hour later. Wanna looked sexier than he ever remembered. She was wearing a one-piece Cavalli fitted dress exposing her beautiful cleavage, a pair of black Gucci pumps, and a black Gucci handbag trimmed in the traditional red and green. She kept it simple on the accessory tip and only wore her mother-of-pearl Rolex and a pair of diamond-studded earrings. Her outfit matched the Maserati, Gran Turismo, with 21-inch, black Asanti rims Champ pulled up in for their date. When Wanna got in the car, she kissed Champ on the lips.

"What's up, boyfriend," she said, in a playful manner.

"Nothing, girlfriend," Champ blurted out, absorbing how good Wanna looked.

"What's wrong, boyfriend," Wanna asked, feeling a little uncomfortable with Champ's assessing look.

"Nothing Wanna, I just never realized how good you look. Give me another one of those kisses."

Champ poked his lips out for Wanna to kiss them. After she kissed him, Champ pulled off as Wanna put in Neyo's *Year of the Gentleman* CD. They drove in silence to the Capital Grill restaurant on Broad Street. Once inside the restaurant, they were seated at a table in the back.

"Hi, my name is Lisa and I'll be your server tonight. Can I get you a drink or an appetizer perhaps?"

Wanna answered without even looking at Champ. "Yes, we'll have the crab legs and cream of spinach dip for our appetizers and apple martinis with double shots of Patron on the rocks," Wanna expertly ordered.

Champ was taken back by how well she knew him, even down to what he would order. When the waitress left, they began to discuss their relationship.

"So, what's it gonna be, Wanna?"

"Whatever you want it to be, Champ. I'm following your lead," she said.

"Listen, Wanna, we didn't just meet. You know me like a book. I never looked at you in this manner and my heart is already involved because you're like a sister to me. If we take our thing any further, my heart will be involved on another level."

As he spoke, Champ looked directly into Wanna's eyes.

"Champ, I'm with you, I have always been and I want to be yours."

"Cool, baby-girl...and the same rules apply. I don't want you involved in my street shit but keep our current, legit businesses."

"Is that all?"

"I just have a few new rules for you. Don't be messing with no lames and you'll be moving out of that house because that nigga Marv been there. Oh, yeah...and have that pussy wet and ready to go whenever I call on it."

Wanna laughed at the last request and said, "I got you, Champ".

Once they finished their meal, they left to go to Champ's crib out in Marcus Hook, PA. This was Champ's four-bedroom, suburban home which no one knew about. Wanna was in awe of the way the house was laid out. The living room furniture matched the off-white paint on the walls and the kitchen was huge with an island and sub-zero appliances. As she looked throughout the house, she noticed that there were built-in flat-screens everywhere, even in the bathroom.

"I love this house. Why haven't I ever been here before?" she asked.

"I just got it, that's why."

"Uh-huh," Wanna mumbled sarcastically.

"Uh-huh, nothing. Let me get another one of them kisses."

"I'll give it to you in the bedroom," Wanna said, as she pointed toward the room. She was tipsy from the drinks she had during dinner but she was well aware of what she was doing.

"That's what I'm talking about," Champ said, as he took her hand and led her to the bedroom. Once inside the room, he hit a button on the wall and a Maxwell CD came pouring out of the surround-sound speakers on the wall.

Wanna didn't give Champ a chance to say anything. She grabbed him by the back of his head and kissed him on the lips. She wanted to assure him that she was ready to takes things further so she began to put her tongue in his mouth. While kissing passionately, they began to undress. They stole glances at each other's naked body. Champ's body was cut from years of working out and Wanna's was flawless as a result of taking care of herself and not having any children.

Wanna began kissing all over Champ's body sending chills up his spine. She continued until she was below his stomach line. The soft wetness of her lips made him hope that she would suck his dick and, within minutes, it was a reality. She started off slowly licking the tip of his dick. The moistness of her mouth made Champ become fully erect. Wanna inserted about six inches of his dick into her mouth. She was going up and down on his dick very slowly, making sure she didn't scrape him with her teeth.

As she glanced up at him, she noticed what she was doing was exciting Champ. She knew she had him where she wanted him, but she wanted to make sure she was pleasing him like no other. She glided her head all the way down the shaft of his dick and stuck her tongue out to gently lick his balls. The wetness of her tongue made Champ back up a little and let out a 'Damn'. His reaction made Wanna became more aggressive and began to suck faster and harder, which made Champ lose control.

Wanna felt him tensing up as the head of his dick started to throb. She knew he was about to cum, so she continued to suck his dick aggressively until he exploded in her mouth. She was sure to swallow every drop as she kept sucking and licking the tip of his dick.

Champ sighed as he lifted her up and pushed her back on the bed. She licked her lips as she looked up at him with much desire showing in her eyes. She lifted her hand toward her mouth as she licked two of her fingers. She slowly glided them down her body as she opened up her legs to touch herself. Champ watched and was turned on by the show. She lifted up her foot and gently rubbed it up and down his leg. Her sighs and moans were too much for Champ. He pushed her leg aside leaning over Wanna's naked body.

He began to suck on the nipples of her perfect, brown titties and slowly made his way down to her belly button. She was squirming and her pussy was wet from every touch. Champ started to lick her pussy and could taste her juices. He took his middle finger and inserted it deep inside her as she began to whisper out his name. Wanna was so turned on by Champ and the way he licked her pussy that she climaxed within minutes. Champ could feel her legs shaking as they closed in around his head. He lifted up and pushed her leg back as he inserted his dick inside her tight, wet pussy.

"Damn, daddy, this dick is good...please don't stop," Wanna moaned.

She thought of this moment for a long time but she never imagined it would be this good. She became so caught up in her emotions that tears of joy began to flow down her cheeks.

Champ fucked her long and hard all through the night. This was the first time in 35 years that Wanna ever felt pure ecstasy. After Champ busted his third nut, and Wanna's sixth, they laid there together in their own juices. Wanna rested her head on Champ's chest; this was where she wanted to be for the rest of her life.

Chapter 3

Tone woke up with one thing on his mind, and that was to do Rocky dirty. He had convinced himself that Rocky was playing him. He never considered the fact that he had been fucking Rocky over since they first started doing business. Tone always gave his customers beat-up work and charged them the maximum dollar. Even when he saw the brick that Bam got back from Rocky, he didn't identify his work from its stamp the way most brick pushers did. Instead, he noticed that it was his by how dull and whacked up it looked. In Tone's mind, he was being fair to Rocky and Rocky was being slick.

"Where the fuck is the nigga Bam at?" Tone wondered aloud, as he began to re-evaluate his situation. *At times like this, I wish I still had Ducky on the squad. Both he and Bam will kill on the spot, but Ducky is always on time. In fact, he's normally early. But, fuck Ducky, he's all up Champ's ass,* Tone thought. He was so consumed by his thoughts that he didn't realize Bam had walked up to the car. Bam banged on the window, scaring the hell out of Tone making him even madder. Tone jumped out of the car.

"Don't bang on my fucking car like that…and why are you always late?" he asked, sternly.

"Man it's 10:05, I'm only five minutes late," said Bam, who was in no way feeling chumped by Tone's cold stare.

"Man, whatever…let's just get in this greasy spoon jawn and discuss our plans," Tone said, as he walked toward Champions.

"I'm going to tell Champ you called his breakfast store a greasy spoon joint."

Bam knew exactly how to get under Tone's skin.

"Fuck Champ, that pussy knows I'm not the fucking one."

"You know, Champ used to box and he's still nice with his hands."

Bam knew that Tone would start hating on Champ the way he always did.

"I never gave a fuck about that fighting shit. That nigga knows who to try that fake-ass Floyd Mayweather shit with."

Tone turned from Bam and walked toward the store. Bam knew he had Tone pissed off but he did that at times to make Tone express how he really felt about niggas. Tone would talk about Champ and other niggas that he was supposed to be cool with like a dog when they weren't around. However, when in their presence, he would be all up in their face like it was all good. Bam loved Tone, but that was the one thing he didn't like about him.

As they walked into the restaurant, they were greeted by their server.

"Welcome to Champions. My name is Rhonda and I'll be serving you today."

Rhonda smiled, revealing white teeth as she turned to lead them to their table.

"Damn, this little bitch is bad," Tone whispered to Bam as he admired Rhonda's fat ass rocking back and

forth as her five-foot, four-inch body led them to their
seats.

"Can I get y'all something to drink?" Rhonda asked.

Tone looked at Rhonda as if he wanted to eat her as he
answered.

"Yeah, two ice teas with lemon and we are ready to
order our food."

"Sure, go ahead."

"We'll have two platters with turkey bacon, scrambled
eggs, and home fries, with two side orders of pancakes."

"Sure, and I'll be right back with your drinks," Rhonda
said, with a smile.

"Take your time, Renee," Tone said, forgetting her
name already.

"That's Rhonda," she said, still smiling.

"I'm sorry, but I did know that it started with an R."

Rhonda left and within minutes returned with their
beverages. They got their food 15 minutes later as they
started to map out how to get at Rocky.

"Bam, I want you to call the nigga and tell him to meet
you so you can grab some work off of him this evening.
Make sure it's right before it gets dark outside," Tone told
him.

"Suppose the nigga don't want to meet me?" asked
Bam.

"Then we'll go meet him," Tone said, putting a piece
of turkey bacon in his mouth.

"We? I told him we were on the outs, so he'll think I'm
on some funny shit if I say we are going to meet him,"
Bam said, sipping his ice tea.

"You're going to act like you're coming alone, but
we're both going to pop up on him...then we're going to
snatch the snake nigga up, torture him, and rob his snake

ass," Tone said, as he ate the last of his pancakes and sipped on his ice tea.

"Okay, that's the plan," Bam said, while thinking to himself that Tone was the biggest snake he ever met.

"Can I get y'all some coffee, a slice of pie, or something?" Rhonda asked, as she began to clear their plates from the table.

Tone shook his head, "Nah, just bring us the check."

"Here you go, fellas. I'll take it when you're ready."

Rhonda took the check out of her book and placed it on the table.

"Here you go," Tone said, giving her a 50-dollar bill for their $18 meal without even looking at the amount of the check.

"I'll get your change."

"Keep the change. When you want to hang up that apron, let Champ know to call his boss, Big Tone, and I'll make sure you never work again."

Tone wished that Champ actually worked for him but he had no problem lying to get what he wanted.

"Sure," Rhonda said, smiling more at the tip she received than at Tone. Tone got up and walked out with Bam following him. Rhonda stood at the table saying to herself, *Fucking cornball with all that jewelry on looking like a rapper early in the morning.*

As soon as they got outside, Bam called Rocky. Tone waited impatiently, ear-hustling the conversation.

"What'd he say?" Tone said, as soon as Bam hung up the phone.

"He said that he would hit me tomorrow and that he got something nice for me," Bam said, thinking about how he came up hustling with Rocky. They were cool until Tone decided to play divide and conquer with his childhood homies.

"Damn, that nigga must got some more shit coming in tomorrow, that fucking snake," Tone said. "Well...we'll see tomorrow."

"Yeah, we'll see," said Bam, as the two shook hands and promised to get together the next day.

~~~~~

Sharon and Wanna went to the King of Prussia Mall to do some shopping. Sharon had to admit that Wanna had a new glow to her already. She talked to Sharon all day about Champ; first thing in the morning on the phone, on the ride to the mall, and now while they were shopping. She gave Sharon every detail about their night, especially the sex. The only thing she didn't expose was that she was at Champ's house and where the house was located because he told her not to mention it to anyone. Wanna followed what Champ told her and didn't mention the crib.

Champ's decision not to tell Sharon where he lived was nothing personal. Champ had love for Sharon and Micky, and trusted Ern's wife and their son, but he didn't trust Tone as far as he could throw him. He always heard the slick hatin' shit Tone said about him but he never tripped because he knew that Tone would never come straight at him. Besides, that sideways shit was always bitch-shit to him.

"Girl, that nigga is a winner for real!" Wanna said.

"Girl, I'm happy for you, but you're not going to Champ me to death," Sharon said, as they rode up the escalator in Neiman Marcus to the women's department.

"Bitch, I let you Tone me to death. Pretty Tone this, Pretty Tone that," Wanna said, with a smile on her face.

Sharon smiled back without sincerity. Wanna, knowing her girl, could sense that there was something wrong.

"I'm just joking, Sharon. You know I don't mind how much you talk about Tone to me. You're my girl, and I'll always listen," Wanna said, with compassion.

"Wanna, I ain't tripping about what you said about me talking to you all the time about Tone. I'm thinking about how people look at me and the rumors surrounding Ern's death. It's been on my mind every since that hating bitch, Meeka, told me that people put my name in those nasty rumors surrounding my husband's murder," Sharon said, with tears in her eyes.

"I told you that bitch, Meeka, is a hater. I never heard that rumor," Wanna said, trying to appease her best girlfriend.

"You're right, and I'm done with that bitch. She can never touch this good shit again," Sharon said, wiping her tears and swinging her hair back.

"You can let Dana do your hair. You'll like it because Dana don't be having all of that gossip shit in her shop," Wanna said, trying to ease Sharon's pain.

"I swear I didn't have anything to do with Ern's death. I loved Ern! I know I fucked up by getting involved with Tone, but what can I do? I fucking love this man, too. My whole life is crazy!"

By this time, the tears were starting to flow down Sharon's face. Wanna hugged her friend in the middle of the department store while Sharon regained her composure.

"Sharon, you're good people, and Ern knows that you mean well and you never had intentions on fucking with Tone. That shit just happened," Wanna said, trying to pacify her friend. But as she listened to her rationalization, she realized just how fucked up it was that Tone and Sharon were together. Sharon got herself under control, so they could shop and enjoy the rest of their day together. Sharon knew without a doubt that Wanna had her back and that relieved her.

"So, what did Champ do to you that got you glowing?" Sharon asked, once again sounding like herself.

"Girl, what didn't he do? I never came so much and so hard in my life," Wanna said, with her eyes closed as if trying to replay the events of last night in her head.

"Yeah, was it that good, girl?"

"Sharon, that nigga got a honey wheat hoagie roll in his draws."

They both burst out laughing.

"Damn girl...it's like that?"

They enjoyed the rest of the day shopping and talking about their men.

Chapter 4

Champ woke up to the smell of breakfast in the air. He didn't know what was cooking, but he knew it smelled good. It made him think of his last girlfriend, April. April was gorgeous, but she wouldn't cook or clean. The pussy was good, but her stuck-up ass was only good at being pretty. The thoughts of April made Champ start comparing her to Wanna, and it turned out that Wanna was a far better woman. Wanna had a good job working with mentally challenged children and she owned several properties with Champ already as a result of their brother/sister relationship. She carried herself like a woman and she dressed her ass off. Some would say that April was prettier since she had an exotic look; her dad was Puerto Rican and her mom was Black which contributed to her long hair and dominate features. Wanna was pretty as well and, now that Champ had the chance to get some of that good pussy, he realized that there was no comparison. Wanna was by far the best woman. In the middle of his thoughts, Wanna appeared in the doorway of the bedroom barefoot, wearing some boy shorts and a bra.

"Brush your teeth and wash your face, sleepy head. I made breakfast."

"Okay, lil' sis, I'll be right down," Champ said, being smart.

"I'm not your damn sister!" Wanna snapped, causing her nose to flare up, making her look even more sexy.

"My fault, baby," Champ said, walking towards her with his arms stretched out for a hug wearing nothing but his Polo boxer briefs. Seeing the impression of his morning hardness made Wanna forget she was mad. She walked up to him and cuddled up to her man before kissing him on the lips.

"You're either nasty or you just simply love me because you kissed my lips and I still have morning breath," Champ said, as he walked toward the bathroom.

"Whatever, nigga! You should be happy that I kissed you at all," Wanna said, trying to sound gangster as she walked downstairs.

Champ was surprised when he saw how much food she had cooked for him. She made a spread that consisted of cheese grits, beef sausage, turkey scrapple, pancakes, eggs, and honey-wheat biscuits.

"Damn, what are you trying to do, get me fat?"

"No...I'm doing my job. If you gain a pound or two in the process, we can work it off. Know what I mean?" Wanna said, as she uncrossed and crossed her legs giving Champ a glimpse at her camel foot pussy print poking through her boy shorts.

"Yeah, is that right?" he said, looking at her as he began to eat. As they ate, they talked about everything from life to sports to what was going on in their old West Philly neighborhood.

"How was your day at the mall with Sharon?" asked Champ.

"It was cool."

"How is she doing?" Champ asked, before sipping on his juice.

"She's good. She's stressing because the rumors about Ern's murder are coming up again and they put her name in the shit now."

"Word, who?"

"Hating-ass Meeka from 38th and Mount Vernon Street," Wanna replied.

"Where did she get that from?"

"I don't know. Personally, I think the bitch made it up herself."

"They know Sharon didn't have shit to do with that. She loved that nigga, Ern," Champ said.

"Yeah, I know and she's really stressed out about how she got caught up with Tone."

"That nigga took advantage of her grief, and basically said fuck his friendship with Ern."

"That's some dirty shit and now my girl is looking crazy."

"On some real shit, that nigga is the one that is looking crazy. He's looking like he wanted to be Ern his entire life, and that's why I don't trust him."

Wanna nodded her head in agreement as she took another piece of scrapple.

"Listen to this funny shit. When I went passed the breakfast store yesterday, this new young girl that Ms. Gail hired asked to speak to me. She said that this fake rapper look-alike with a bunch of junk jewelry on named Big Tone said that he's my boss," Champ told her. They both started laughing.

"This nigga is losing his mind!" Champ blurted out between laughs.

Wanna decided to change the subject, so she eased over to the stool that Champ was sitting on and started to kiss him. He was so wrapped up in the kisses that he didn't realize she had turned him away from the table. Wanna reached her hand down into his boxers and pulled out his dick. He was already semi-hard so there wasn't much work for her to do. She took a sip from his glass of orange juice making sure to let a cube of ice slip into her mouth. She kissed his lips once again before she kneeled down to suck his dick. The mixture of the warmth of her mouth and the coolness of the ice combined with the saliva dripping down his balls made Champ lose his mind.

"Damn, Wanna, this feels so good!" Champ said, through clinched teeth.

Wanna let out a moan and continued to please her man. Once Champ was fully erect, he pulled his dick out of her mouth, picked her up, and put her on a clear space on the table. Wanna balanced herself as he removed her panties and slid his dick into her wet pussy. She was already on the verge of coming just from sucking his dick. She had never been this turned on by a man.

"Fuck me, daddy, fuck me! Oooh, right there, right there," She exclaimed, while digging her nails down his back. He didn't care because he was enjoying himself.

Wanna's pussy was so tight around his dick and it got wetter with each stroke. The sound of the plates moving on the table aroused her even more. She leaned up to Champ's ear and told him that she was about to explode. Upon hearing this, Champ dug into her deeper causing her to fall back down on the table. Champ started long-dicking Wanna until she came all over him and the table.

"Damn, you're a nasty nigga!" she said, jokingly, knowing that she enjoyed every moment of what just happened.

~~~~~

Bam and Tone were on their way to meet Rocky at 41st Street and Parkside Avenue. Rocky told Bam that he had something far better than the last time. Bam even reconsidered letting Rocky live for a minute. He was going to tell Tone that Rocky wasn't ready to meet and instead go meet him alone. He was going to inform Rocky of Tone's plan, but he decided to go ahead and roll with Tone's plan. He told Tone the time and place Rocky suggested they meet and they were on their way.

"You know, we can just take Rocky shit. We don't have to kill his bitch ass," Bam said, feeling like the snake he was for crossing Rocky because of Tone's jealousy.

"It's not about taking no money. I have a lot of money. This is about Rocky trying to play me, so now we got to rock Rocky," Tone said, laughing at his little "rock Rocky" joke.

"Fuck it, I'm with you," Bam said. Although he acted like he was riding with Tone, he was really thinking, *Yeah...you have money, not me. It's all about you.*

As they pulled up on Parkside Avenue, Bam dialed Rocky's phone. When Rocky answered, Bam let him know that he was in a black Marauder with dark tent. They knew Rocky would piss on himself when he got in the car and saw Tone with a burner in his hand.

"Damn, where is this nigga at?" Tone said, after waiting for about ten minutes.

"I'll call him back," Bam said, pushing the redial button on his phone.

"This nigga ain't..."

Boom, Boom, Boom!

The sound was a riot pump dumping into the Marauder from a van that pulled up beside them before Bam could finish his sentence. Tone was hit in the left shoulder and, without hesitation, he raised his gun and started busting back. By then the van had disappeared into the park.

"Put this motherfucker in drive!" Tone yelled to Bam. When he looked over, he noticed Bam slumped over the steering wheel and knew he had to get out of there. He got out of the car, went around to the driver side, opened the door, and pushed Bam's body out onto the street.

Bam's blood was everywhere. The look on his face was one of total fear and shock. He never imagined he was being set up.

"Don't leave me, don't leave me." Bam used his last bit of strength to plead with Tone.

Tone jumped in the driver seat and backed out, feeling a bump under the tire.

"Oh shit, I think I hit the nigga. Fuck it…he's dying anyway," Tone said aloud to himself, pulling out now and running Bam's body over completely. He sped through the park and down Kelly drive. He pulled off the drive onto Fairmount Avenue heading for Micky's house.

Micky was already waiting for Tone because Tone called him to say he was on his way. When Tone pulled the battered Marauder into the garage, Micky knew there was something wrong. When Micky saw Tone covered in blood with his left shoulder hanging, he got nervous.

"Take me to the hospital. I've been shot!" Tone shouted to Micky.

"Who did it?" Micky asked.

"I don't know who did it, but Rocky was behind it," Tone said, as Micky helped him into his Lexus LS460.

"Rocky, I thought he was your young bull?" Micky said, now confused.

"I'll explain later. Hurry up and get me to the hospital! Call your mom and tell her what hospital we're going to. I also need you to go get my little cousin, Toot, and let him get rid of this car," Tone said. All while his left arm felt like it was on fire.

Micky got to Hahnemann Hospital at Broad and Vine in seven minutes flat.

Chapter 5

Sharon spent the night at the hospital. She was waiting for Wanna to come so she could use her friend's shoulder to lean on. It was a long night. Word of Tone getting shot traveled fast. The rumors started to surface throughout the hood and people were coming in and out of the lobby to find out what happened to Tone. Some were coming out of concern while others were there just to be newsy. Sharon didn't know half the people who were coming there nor did she care. She knew how the streets were, and her sole concern was on Tone and her son. Micky came in and out of the hospital three or four times to check on his mom and Tone. Micky told his mom to call him when the doctors cleared Tone for visitors.

Tone was scheduled for surgery this morning and the doctor told Sharon, his mom, Bernadette, and his sister, Nay, that he had nerve damage and there was a possibility that his arm would have to be amputated at the shoulder. Bernadette had love for Sharon, but Nay only got along with her on the strength of her brother. They all talked with each other a little, but for the most part Sharon kept her distance because she knew how loud and ghetto Nay could get and this wasn't the time or the place. When Wanna came into the lobby, she went up and hugged Sharon. Sharon knew that she was the one person besides

Micky and Tone that truly cared about her. Wanna was always there for Sharon.

"Sharon, are you okay?"

"Yeah, I'm holding on. I just want Tone to be okay," Sharon said, with tears in her eyes.

"Tone will be okay. He's strong," Wanna said, in an attempt to console her friend. Just then, the doctor came out.

"May I speak to Mrs. Davis, please?" he said, looking in Sharon's direction. Sharon excused herself from Wanna and walked over to the doctor who was already standing next to Bernadette and Nay.

"Ladies, Anthony is a strong man. He made it through the surgery, but he still has no movement in his left arm. He has severe nerve damage to the shoulder and amputation is still a possibility."

"Ain't nobody amputating nothing on my brother," Nay said, going into her ghetto act and embarrassing the hell out of Sharon.

"Calm down," Bernadette said to her daughter, while trying to keep her mouth shut. The doctor looked on before he continued.

"Anthony can have visitors now, but remember he's heavily sedated and he needs his rest. I ask that you keep the visits brief and only two people in the room at a time."

The doctor walked away as a nurse led the way for Bernadette and Nay, who had bumped Sharon out of the way so that she would have to wait. Sharon hated the little, ignorant bitch, but she kept her cool and went back to talk to Wanna.

As she approached, she overheard Wanna checking Meeka.

"Don't come around my girl friend with all the gossiping and negativity. She's got enough on her mind as it is without you being newsy and feeding her a bunch of bull shit," Wanna said, in a low but stern voice to Meeka, who was standing there looking dumb because she knew Wanna was telling the truth. Meeka didn't come out of concern for a friend, and she damn sure wasn't there worried about Tone. Her only motive for being there was to be newsy.

"Calm down, Wanna. What's wrong?" Sharon said, as she walked up catching the end of the conversation.

"No...I'm just tired of these bitches acting like they're concerned about you but knowing in their hearts that they don't give a fuck about you," Wanna said, breathing fire.

"I didn't mean to say anything to upset nobody. I was just telling you what the streets were saying. Sharon, I'll see you at the shop tomorrow," Meeka said, without waiting for a response before she walked out the door. Wanna turned to look at Sharon.

"Sharon, stay away from that bitch! She's no good for you."

"I already told you that I'm done with her. But what just happened?" Sharon asked.

"This bitch came over here while you were talking to the doctor. She said she heard that Bam and Tone got killed last night. I told the bitch that I didn't know Bam nor did I know what happened. She then proceeded to say that the streets were saying that Tone left Bam for dead. I just flipped and started cursing the bitch out." Although Wanna was upset, she maintained a low voice that only Sharon could hear.

"I'm changing my number and when Tone gets better he's got to change his lifestyle," Sharon said, looking at her girl friend.

~~~~~

Rocky sat there waiting for Shy and Boop to come to his apartment on Fifth Street at Fairmount Avenue. Rocky wasn't with the gunplay but he wasn't a dummy. He knew that Bam was trying to set him up. Bam told him in one breath that Tone cut him off. He almost believed it until Teddy called and said that Tone came around asking Bingo a lot of questions while with Bam. Rocky knew that Bam was a puppet for Tone and that Tone was vicious. He couldn't meet Bam the first day because he needed Shy and Boop to put in some work for him, but they were tied up with handling something up Frankford where they both grew up.

Knocks on the door startled Rocky.

"Who is it?" Rocky said, irritated.

"Nigga, it's us," Boop said, covering the peephole with his finger so Rocky couldn't see them.

"You niggas play too much," Rocky said, letting them in.

"Shut up!" Boop said, as he punched Rocky in the stomach in a playful manner.

"What's up, niggas?"

"Ain't shit," Shy blurted out, finally breaking his silence.

"What's the verdict?" Boop asked, as he looked in the refrigerator.

"Man, they said that Bam got killed. It was all over the news and they said that he was not only shot but run over by a car, too," Rocky said, as Shy started laughing.

"Yo, somebody else was in that car. After I dumped on the driver side, somebody started busting back from the passenger seat. When we pulled back around through the park the car was gone, but we saw nut-ass Bam in the middle of the street, dead," Boop said, drinking a soda he got from the fridge.

"That had to be nut-ass Tone because everybody's been talking about him getting shot last night. They said he had surgery today and that his left arm is dead," Rocky said, with a confused look on his face.

"Fuck Tone! I told you old-head was a nut years ago and to let us rob him. You were steady saying that he was good people and he be looking out for you. Now we got to rock this nut-ass nigga," Boop shouted out from the kitchen, as he looked for a snack.

"It ain't that easy. I sent newsy-ass Meeka down there to see what was being said. The rumors are floating but ain't nobody say my name. They are linking Bam's murder to Tone's shooting, so Tone probably knows that Bam was meeting me and he's going to be on point," Rocky said.

"Nigga, you sound like you're scared of this fake-ass, Tone Loc looking nigga. I don't give a fuck if old-head is on point. You heard what Biggie said, 'Niggas bleed just like us'," Boop shouted from the kitchen.

"I'm not scared of him or no other nigga. I just don't sleep on niggas and you might not know this, but Tone is known for putting work in, so we got to get him and get him fast," Rocky said, seriously.

"Listen here, Rocky...we're from Frankford where young niggas kill their old-heads all the time. We're going to shoot this nigga until he catch on fire," Shy said.

"Fuck that nigga, Tone. I'm the Boopster," Boop added.

Rocky knew that Boop was about his work. Whenever somebody gave Rocky some problems, he would call his little cousin and his homie, Shy. Boop and Shy would shoot any nigga in broad daylight with no hesitation and they would enjoy it. Rocky wasn't scared of Tone, but he knew Tone would come at them hard so he didn't want Boop or Shy to sleep on Tone.

"All I'm saying is that we need to get Tone as soon as he gets out of the hospital," Rocky said to Boop and Shy, who both agreed. They all shook hands before Boop and Shy headed back to Frankford.

Chapter 6

Tone was awake and aware of what was going on and what had happened. He wasn't sweating his dead arm, which was actually the last thing on his priority list. He told the doctor that he only wanted to allow five people to visit his room - Sharon, Micky, Toot, his mom, and Sab. He refused to see his sister, Nay, after she put on a show in front of the hospital staff. She called Sharon all types of bitches and told him that he was a sucker for letting Sharon handle everything for him. He smacked Nay with his right hand.

"Fuck You, Tone," Nay yelled, just before security stepped in to escort her out of the hospital.

As she left, Nay threatened to go to Tone's apartment in the Northeast and take the CLS-55 that he bought but put in her name.

"Pussy, you gonna hit me?... And you pick that bitch over me?" Nay cried out, tears streaming down her face as she struggled against the guards, "You can keep that bitch cuz I'm takin' the other bitch," she tossed back, referring to his CLS. She knew he couldn't report the car stolen because it was technically hers.

He wasn't concerned with the car because he had bigger fish to fry. He was waiting on his man, Sab, from Camden, New Jersey, to come so that Micky and his cousin, Toot, could show Sab what Rocky looked like and places he was known to frequent.

Sab was Tone's go-to man when shit got thick in Philly. Tone only dealt with Sab when his local boys couldn't handle a situation. Tone knew that Teddy was dying to go at it with him for years now and, because Rocky was fucking with Teddy, Tone felt it was time to make Teddy's wish come true. Because of the paper and power Bingo was building, Tone knew this shit would get too thick for his local crew. Sab and his wild-ass Camden crew was Tone's best shot at winning.

Sab met Tone when he was locked up in Camden County. Tone was there for the weekend and Sab was his cellmate. Sab had already been there for two months before Tone arrived. He told Tone about how he had put in some work for some niggas who let him sit over five stacks. Tone needed Sab for a plan he was cooking up at the time, so he promised Sab he would post his bail when he got out. Tone posted Sab's bail the day after he was released, and for the last five years Sab had been loyal to Tone.

Every time Sab came over the Ben Franklin Bridge to put in some work for Tone somebody died. Tone was sitting in bed thinking of where Rocky got the heart to make a move on him or Bam. He kept coming up with Teddy. Bam's face kept popping up in his head and he kept hearing Bam's voice saying 'Don't leave me'. The scene kept replaying in his head over and over. Tone was going to make sure Rocky paid for killing Bam. *I know his bitch-ass ain't pull the trigger. He probably got his cousin, Boop, to do it. That nigga, Boop, is ruthless but fuck it, now it's on,* he thought.

Tone was pulled from his thoughts when the door opened and Micky walked into the room. Micky really loved Tone; he was all he had as a father figure.

"What's up, Tone, how are you feeling?" Micky asked him.

"Micky, I feel like shit! I'm lying in this bed and I probably won't be able to go to Bam's funeral," Tone said, watching Micky.

"His funeral isn't until this weekend and it's only Monday, so you got like a week," Micky said, trying to be optimistic.

"Baby-boy, they said I'll be here for about two weeks."

"Well, I'll be here every day to check on you. Whatever you need, I'll be sure to get for you."

Tone was a little selfish but he did regret putting Micky in the game. When Micky first asked Tone to get in the game, Tone said no flat out. Micky assured Tone that he was going to do his thing with or without his help so Tone decided to take him under his wing. He showed Micky the game first-hand. He gave Micky the best prices and he never cut his work. He was firm with Micky about staying low key and making sure his mom never found out anything. Sharon would snap if she knew Tone was supplying her son with bricks. Micky sat in the hospital's cheap chair staring at Tone as if he could see the emotions running through Tone's face.

"What's on your mind, Tone?"

"Micky, I don't want you in the middle of this shit. I don't want you hustling until this shit is all over. Once you show my man where Rocky is and what he and Boop look like, I just want you to fall back."

"Okay, Tone, but I can ride on Rocky's bitch-ass by myself."

"Listen Micky, I don't want you nowhere near this shit," Tone said firmly, as the door opened and Toot and Sab walked in.

"Toot, you and Micky wait outside for a minute and I'll send Sab out to get y'all in a few," Tone said, after greeting them.

"Damn, big homie, what happened to you and what do you need me to do?" Sab asked, full of energy reminding Tone of DMX with the way he talked and moved his hands.

"Some little niggas killed my man and hit me. I want you to bring your crew over and handle these niggas. I mean, I want you to do them dirty," Tone spat, with death in his eyes.

"I'm on it. Just tell me where I can find these niggas," Sab said, looking with his one good eye at Tone. His other eye was glass as a result of being stabbed in the eye in high school.

"My people will show you around today and y'all can come through Philly starting tomorrow and get at them niggas."

"I'm cool with that."

"Go get Toot and Micky from outside so I can tell them what to do," Tone directed him. Sab went out into the hallway to get them. Once they came back into the room, Tone got right down to business.

"Show him where Rocky and Boop stay at up Frankford. Don't let the day go by without showing him what Rocky and that nigga, Boop, look like," Tone said, pointing toward Sab with his good hand.

~~~~~

Champ was taking Wanna out to eat, but had to stop by Bingo's pool hall for a quick conversation. Bingo called him and told him that he wanted to talk to him face to face. Champ heard the rumors of what was going on with Rocky, Teddy, Tone, and Bam. Champ grew up with Tone and Bingo and was still cool with both of them. Although he had a little more respect and was a little closer to Bingo than he was to Tone, he decided to stay neutral. He intended to try to defuse the situation so that Sharon and Micky wouldn't have to endure another grieving period if Tone got his goofy ass shot again or even killed.

"Do you want to come in or do you want to stay in the car? I have to talk to Bingo real quick. I'll be back in about 15 minutes," Champ told Wanna.

"I'll wait in the car. I want to call Sharon anyway."

"Okay, I'll make it fast," Champ said, hopping out of the car and walking into the pool hall.

Everybody was playing pool, video poker, and flirting while a jukebox played tunes in the background. Teddy noticed Champ first and ran over to shake Champ's hand.

"Damn, big bro, what's up with that light-skin chick, Kita, you put me on at your party?"

"I don't know, but she told me she called you," Champ said, shaking Teddy's hand.

"She did, but I lost my phone after that," Teddy told him.

"I'll catch up with her for you. Where is your brother?"

"He's in his office, go on back," Teddy said, pointing to the back of the room where the office was located.

Everybody loved Champ and respected him. He treated everybody well and always had time for even the lowest man on the totem pole if he knew him. They said their hello's and hugged.

"Damn, brother, you don't go home to that beautiful wife of yours?" Champ said, referring to his cousin, Thelma, that Bingo married a year ago.

"You know your crazy-ass cousin makes sure I'm at the crib every night," Bingo said, laughing.

"Well, why are you down here with the hard-headed crowd when you should be enjoying your life with your wife not just with your paper?" Champ asked, giving Bingo the hint that Thelma called him complaining about him not spending time with her.

"Champ, I'm grinding and, with this latest bullshit Tone pulled off, I got to tighten up my ship," Bingo said, pouring himself a shot of Patron.

"What's the use of grinding and not enjoying it? Teddy and them can run this pool hall. At our age, we are supposed to be falling back after dark."

"I agree but I'm a workaholic. I bust my ass at the tire shop and in here," Bingo said, sipping his drink.

"Naw, you're not a workaholic. I'm just telling you that, at the end of the day, you should enjoy your money and your wife."

Bingo knew Thelma must have called Champ. He knew Champ was too smooth to just come out and tell him how to handle his wife or what she told him. Bingo decided to leave the home-life conversation alone and instead began to discuss the matter at hand.

"Champ, this faggot-ass nigga, Tone, came to my tire shop asking me about me doing business with a young bull that I don't deal with. He's Teddy's customer, but I don't owe Tone no answers and now this shit may get out of hand and draw on me getting my paper."

"I heard the rumors about what happened but I don't want to take sides," said Champ.

"I just don't want you to be mad if the nigga keep faking crazy and get offed," Bingo responded.

"I hope y'all can work it out. You know how Tone is…I don't pay him no mind when he acts like I owe him something. I just tell his goofy ass to get out of my face, but if shit gets ugly, I'm minding my business. The nigga don't listen to nobody, so I'm not even going to try to talk to him," Champ said, fed up at the fact that Tone was always in the middle of something.

"I was just seeing how you feel about it, but my mind is made up."

"Brother, do you. I don't want to know shit!" Champ said, as he hugged Bingo to leave.

"Hey, Thelma told me you and Wanna are together now."

"Yeah, I got caught up," Champ said, exposing his white teeth with his smile.

"She's a winner."

"I know," Champ said, walking out the door.

When he got back into the car, Wanna was still on the phone with Sharon.

"Where you want to go eat at, Wanna?"

"We can go home and eat leftovers. I just want to be with my man."

"That's cool, I'm tired anyway," Champ said, as he turned up his Brian McKnight CD when Wanna hung up the phone and drove to their home to lie down with peace of mind.

Chapter 7

Sab and his man, Dave, from Camden were sitting outside Rocky's apartment since eight a.m. They had been waiting for two hours for him to come out. They knew Rocky was in the crib because his car was there. Micky showed them the apartment and the car last night, as well as the usual spots he and Boop could be found. They chose to come to Rocky's apartment first because it was closest and, to their surprise, it was where Rocky stayed last night. They could see movement in the apartment. They hoped it wouldn't be long before he surfaced.

"Damn, I feel like a cop on a stake out," Sab said, drinking his coffee from Dunkin' Donuts and eating a glazed doughnut.

"Yeah...but we're not here to protect, we are here to wreck," Dave replied, smoking his Newport and sipping coffee.

"We might have to kill that crackhead that's been sleeping in the hallway, too," Sab said, pointing to some dirty looking man lying on the foyer floor.

The man was overdressed, which was probably his means of keeping warm in the streets.

"Fuck it...we can put him out of his misery, too," Dave said, agreeing with Sab.

"Yeah, we'll be doing him a favor, but we'll only shoot him if he gets in our way or gets newsy."

Just then, a brown-skinned chick came outside and put a bag in Rocky's car.

"You see that?" Dave said, hyped up and sitting on the edge of his seat.

"Yeah, be cool and let's see what happens," Sab said, placing his hand over Dave's chest to calm him down.

The girl went back inside the apartment. She came back out ten minutes later, but this time she was accompanied by Rocky. When they were outside the door, Sab and Dave started walking toward the couple. At the sight of the two strangers, Rocky had a bad feeling that he got caught slipping and considered running back into the apartment for protection. Before Sab or Dave could raise their guns, they were startled by an unexpected occurrence. The man they had presumed to be a crackhead emerged from the building and began blasting Rocky with rapid fire from an A-R assault rifle. He then turned the gun on the girl, whose expression suggested that she knew the shooter, and hit her in the face and upper body until she hit the ground. The shooter then ran down the street not bothering to fire a single shot at either Sab or Dave.

"Damn! Did you see that wild shit?" Dave asked, as he and Sab jumped back into the mini-van they were driving.

"Yeah, that's some strange shit. I'm going to back out of this block because I don't want to startle that trigger happy nigga," Sab said, as he put the van in reverse.

Sab's mind was racing as he replayed the incident. They drove back to Camden to change cars. They were both trying to decipher what happened on Rocky's block.

"Man, what the fuck! Did Tone put a double hit out on this nigga?" Dave asked, trying to get some answers about how and why they lost their target to another nigga.

"I don't know, but let's get in the other wheel and get in touch with Micky," Sab said, turning the ignition off. They jumped into the car that Sab bought with the money Micky gave them. Tone told Micky there was no limit to the expense money that was at Sab's disposal to get the job done.

"Yo, you're border line genius to buy this jawn," Dave said, putting the seat of the yellow taxicab down.

"Yeah, this is some slick shit that a nigga would never see coming," Sab said, admiring his own brilliance.

He called Micky on his way back over the Ben Franklin Bridge. Micky said he would meet them on 17th and Spring Garden Streets in front of Community College. Sab didn't get into it about the so-called crackhead, but he needed to ask Micky a few questions face to face.

"He's meeting us in front of Community College so we can holler at him," Sab said, making a right onto Seventh Street off the bridge.

"Yeah, we need to see what's up with this other nigga taking our target," Dave said, lighting up another cigarette.

"Yeah, we'll get paid regardless, but that shit could have turned ugly if he would've started blasting that A-R at us," Sab said, turning onto Spring Garden Street.

"Yeah, we didn't stand a chance, but it seemed as if dude let us slide. He clearly saw us standing out there," Dave said, still trying to understand it all.

"Yeah you're right. We should have never made it behind that car or back in the van because that A-R is crazy, dawg," Sab replied as he pulled behind Micky's car.

Micky and Toot got out of the car as Dave and Sab exited theirs. They all shook hands and said their 'What's ups'.

"Y'all are crazy as shit, riding around in that cab," Micky said, chuckling. They all started laughing. Sab cut the laughter short, getting down to business.

"Micky, some crazy shit happened when we went to get at that nigga, Rocky. There was some bum-looking crackhead lying in the hallway of Rocky's building. We had the drop on that nigga but, before we knew it, the crackhead started blasting on him and his bitch."

Micky and Toot shared looks of disbelief and confusion.

Toot chimed in, "So...you're saying the nigga got hit, but he got hit by a crackhead."

"I don't know if he was a crackhead, but he looked like one... either that or a bum," Sab explained.

"As long as the bitch-ass nigga, Rocky, is dead! I don't give a damn who the fuck killed him," Micky said.

"It ain't about somebody else putting in the work. I just don't want to be around when somebody is busting because that shit could have gotten messy, especially without us knowing that somebody else was on the job." Sab became frustrated as he explained the situation, mainly because he really wanted to put the work in himself.

"We don't know where dude came from or why he hit the nigga, but we'll tell Tone y'all put the work in," Micky said, knowing Sab was really concerned with what Tone would think.

"That's what's up and we're going up Frankford in a few to try to catch up with this other pussy nigga. If anybody jumps out and tries to do that shit this time we're hitting their ass, too," Sab said. They shook hands and went their separate ways.

While Sab and Dave were on their way to Frankford, Micky and Toot went to the hospital. Toot was full of jokes while riding in the passenger seat.

"Yo...they called you a crackhead, son," Toot said, emphasizing the word "son" to mock Sab's Jersey accent.

"Man that shit ain't funny! Them niggas were supposed to be up Frankford this morning not at Rocky's crib. They are lucky I didn't let that A-R loose on their asses," Micky said, feeling the work he put in but not the crackhead jokes that accompanied it.

Micky and Toot knew that Rocky was a cold bitch. They figured if they killed him at the same time that Sab and Dave got Boop, everything would die down and they could get right back to hustling. They knew Tone would never agree or believe they could put in work, so they planned on killing Rocky themselves.

"I hope they kill that nigga, Boop, quick or you will have to be my getaway driver again," Micky said, seriously wanting to get this shit over with so he could get back to his money, ho's, and clothes.

"Naw, dawg, the next time I'm the crackhead and you're the getaway driver," Toot said, laughing hard as they entered the hospital lobby.

Micky didn't find anything funny. Toot walked back to Tone's room and Micky stopped in the lobby to kick it with Wanna.

"Hey, handsome," Wanna said, hugging Micky.

"What's up, Aunt Wanna?" Micky said, returning the hug.

"How are you doing? You better be staying out of trouble."

"Aunt Wanna, I'm chilling. I just want Tone to be okay and for you and mom to be cool. The only person who makes sure I'm good beside y'all is Uncle Champ," Micky said, being his smooth self.

"We are family," Wanna said, as Sharon walked up.

"What's up, Mom?"

"You, boy, come give me a hug."

Micky hugged and kissed his mom.

"Micky, you want something off the food cart?"

"Naw, Mom, I'm good."

"I want to talk to you later, son."

"Okay, Mom, but I'm about to go see Tone."

"Go ahead, he's been asking about you all day."

Wanna and Sharon turned to go to the food cart as Micky walked down the hall. Although he was concerned about Tone, he was having some impure thoughts. *Damn, Aunt Wanna is up in them jeans. Her ass is getting fat*, he thought to himself as he walked toward Tone's room.

Micky pushed the door open to see Tone sitting there with Toot.

"What's up Tone, what it do?"

"I'm good, little nigga. I'm just waiting to get the fuck out of here."

"Yo, did Toot tell you that the nigga, Rocky, got aired out?"

"Yeah I told y'all my Jersey niggas are hard-body!" Tone said, dick-eating Sab for no reason.

"Yeah, them Jersey niggas are wild," Micky said, knowing damn well he had put the work in.

"And I was going to get the whole crew to come over until he convinced me that he could handle it with Dave alone."

"Them niggas are crazy, son," Toot said, still emphasizing "son" to mock Sab's accent.

"Yo, the news is on. Turn it up," Tone said, scooting up in his bed the best he could.

"We are live on Channel 3. Behind us is the scene of a double homicide that just occurred in the Fairmount District of Philadelphia. It appears that when Tameeka James and Ronald Pew were leaving their apartment at Fourth and Fairmount this morning they were greeted by a gunman. From the looks of the scene and the accounts of neighboring witnesses, the gunman approached them with a high power assault rifle and riddled their bodies with bullets. The Police Chief said that there are no motives and no suspects at the present time. We'll keep you posted as the news of this investigation unfolds. I'm Walt Hunter and this is Channel 3 Eyewitness News."

"Damn, that nigga is sleeping with the maggots," Tone said, taking this time to talk trash about Rocky's murder.

"Damn, I didn't know that he was fucking Meeka," Micky said, remembering how she looked when she noticed it was him behind the trigger of the A-R.

"Yeah, we partied that bitch one day and then he fell in love with her," Tone said, not wanting it to be known that his jealousy played a part in his hatred for Rocky.

"Damn, Tone, how could you be comfortable telling me you were fucking my mom's hairdresser? That bitch has even been to my mom's house," said Micky, mad at Tone for playing his mom. Tone quickly tried to clean up the situation.

"I was drunk when we did it. When she called me the next day I put the bitch in check and she's been kicking it with Rocky ever since."

Tone knew he stuck his foot in his mouth, and he was hoping Micky wouldn't tell Sharon.

"Damn Micky, I know I fucked up, but please don't tell your mom," Tone pleaded.

"Tone, I'm not into running back telling my mom shit that would hurt her. But don't talk about no bitches to me because that's like me playing my mom," Micky said, as he realized for the first time that Tone was a nut.

"I'll remember that, little man," Tone replied.

Toot could feel the tension in the air so he decided to change the subject.

"So...what's the next move?" he asked.

"Once they get Boop, can we get back at this paper?" Micky questioned anxiously.

"Naw...I want you to fall back until I get out of here. There are a few more niggas I want to get at before this shit is clear."

"What niggas are you talking about? Because we can handle it today," Micky said, wanting to get this shit over with.

"This shit is personal! These niggas ain't no walk in the park and who the hell are *we*?" Tone asked, thinking about how he was going to go after Teddy and Bingo.

"We, is me and Toot. We can put work in better than them lame-ass Jersey niggas you got," Micky expressed, with arrogance.

Tone became flustered by Micky's declaration.

"Follow my lead and stay the fuck in y'alls lane. Y'all are hustlers...not fucking killers."

Micky opened his mouth to protest but stopped once he realized his mom was walking into the room. Sharon's presence ruined the flow of conversation. Toot and Micky remained in the room for ten more minutes then left to run a few errands.

Chapter 8

Bam's funeral had come and gone. Tone wanted Boop dead before Bam was buried but Boop had been on point. Tone was going to be released from the hospital in a few days and he didn't want to have to deal with Boop when he got home. He had bigger fish to fry.

Sab promised Tone there would be a news flash last night with Boop being the main topic. Tone was tired of excuses. He wanted the situation handled.

There was an attempt on Boop a couple of days ago but it was unsuccessful because Boop was on point. He had just left his aunt after discussing Rocky's funeral arrangements. When he got back to Frankford, he was driving down Torresdale Avenue and noticed the same cab that had been riding around in the projects for the last few days. The cab was a good way to be discrete, but Sab and Dave both rode in the front seat instead of one in the back as if being taxied. It drew suspicion to the car, which made the ploy less effective. When Boop drove by the cab, he noticed that it pulled out behind him. As he was about to pull onto Dipman Street, he called Shy, who was chilling with his young bulls in the projects, and told him to air out the cab that was following him. When Boop turned the corner, the cab followed as he expected. Boop waited until he saw Shy, then slammed on the brakes damn near causing Sab to crash into him. Shy and about six young bulls started firing at the cab. Sab didn't panic but instead backed all the way off the block. The cab looked like Swiss cheese but Sab and Dave lived to talk about it. After that incident, it was apparent to Sab that Boop was on point when it came to the riding shit. He also knew Tone was getting frustrated with the messages he sent him through Micky and Toot.

Tone sat in his bed dangling his dead arm waiting for Micky and Toot. He was watching the news and started talking to himself.

News flash, huh? What news flash? This nigga, Sab, is getting soft. If I have to kill Boop myself, I'm taking Sab's ass out as well. This nigga even got Micky and Toot laughing at me, he reflected.

His thoughts were cut short when two visitors walked in. He blew out air when he realized that it wasn't Micky and Toot but instead Starsky and Hutch, two local detectives that had been investigating Tone for the last three years. Detective Starks was known in West Philly as Starsky and his partner, Detective Hutson, was known as Hutch. They received the nicknames from the local drug dealers to mock the TV show cops.

"Pretty, mother-fucking Tony," Starks said, when he entered the room.

"What the fuck do y'all want?"

"We wanted to come see our friend," Hutson butted in.

"Well y'all got the wrong fucking room because y'all don't have a friend in here," Tone spat, not giving a fuck about the local detectives because he had one of the best lawyers in Philly.

"You got a lot of mother-fucking mouth for a man with one arm," Starks said, hitting below the belt with the statement.

"I don't care if I have no arms and no toes...as long as I got these big balls and this long horse-dick I'll still get all the bitches, and I'll never be y'alls friend," Tone said, causing both detectives to turn red.

"Well, listen here, Horse Dick. We know the motherfucker who shot you is the same one who killed your homeboy, Bam. If we find enough evidence to prove you were at the scene of the murder we're booking you and then you can use the 'horse dick' on the fags in the joint," Starks yelled in Tone's face.

"Well...when y'all get that *evidence,* call Fred Perri and tell him to call me," Tone said smugly, using his lawyer's name as a threat.

"We'll see you later, you dead-arm bitch," Hutson said, as the detectives left the room.

Tone was mad. He was pissed off about his arm and the fact they were busting on it. Tone already hated Starsky and Hutch but this last encounter made it worse. Detective Hutson really hated all drug dealers no matter their race, especially since his ex-wife overdosed on dope while she was pregnant with their baby.

Micky and Toot entered Tone's room about fifteen minutes after the detectives left. They could see the harsh expression on Tone's face so they knew he was heated about something.

"Damn, big homie, are you okay?" Micky said, reaching his hand out to shake Tone's good hand.

"The mother-fucking cops just left here talking shit. I got to get up out of this fucking hospital," Tone said, shaking Micky's extended hand.

"The cops? What the fuck they want?" Toot said, putting his hand in the air to get the next handshake.

69

"Nut-ass Starsky and Hutch came in here talking about how they know the nigga that shot me is the one who killed Bam and that they are gathering evidence," Tone said, shaking Toot's hand.

"Them cops are some dickheads. They'll do anything to make a case, but they can't put you at the scene of Bam's murder. Besides, Rocky's dead, Bam's dead, the Marauder is burned up, and that nigga Boop will never tell," Micky said, trying to give Tone some words of comfort.

"Yeah, you're right. But I ain't taking no chances with this shit. Tell Sab to bring the whole crew over and get this nigga, Boop. Bam has been buried since yesterday and this nigga Boop is still walking around," Tone spat.

"Cousin, you're not even sure Boop had anything to do with it," Toot chimed in.

"Who else is going to bust their gun for bitch-ass Rocky?" Tone said upset, thinking that Toot was taking up for Boop.

"I don't know if Boop had anything to do with it but, fuck it, he's Rocky's cousin. Whatever it takes for us to get back to our paper we'll do," Micky said, speaking on behalf of him and Toot.

"Get Sab on the phone and tell him I'm not feeling his work right now," Tone told Micky.

"Yo, on some real shit, the nigga, Boop, might be too much for them Jersey niggas to handle. Boop is not going to play victim. He proved that when he aired that nut-ass cab out that them niggas were driving," Micky said.

Tone was quiet. He was thinking about how Micky had grown up so fast and how Micky's gangster swag reminded him of Ern.

"If Sab and them don't get it done within the next 24 hours, I want y'all to get our little bottom squad on it," Tone said, looking from Micky to Toot and back to Micky.

"We're about to go meet Sab now and I'll let him know you're unhappy with him," Micky said.

They shook hands with Tone and were on their way to meet Sab who met them at Haddon and Spruce in front of the Masjid in Camden. After brief greetings, Micky went right into what Tone told him to say.

"Sab, I don't know what you need to get this job done, but the big guy said he's not happy with this shit. He wants it to be over tonight or at least in the next 24 hours."

"Tell big cat I got it. I had the nigga last night but the cops came down the street and I had to get out of there," Sab said, looking at Micky with his good eye.

"He said to bring your whole crew over because this shit is getting out of control."

"Okay, Micky, we're on it."

"Do y'all need extra vehicles or burners?"

"Naw, we're good. This shit is personal now. They aired my cab out and they got my man losing faith in me," Sab said, as they all shook hands and parted ways.

On the way back over the bridge, Micky called Champ. Champ told him he'd meet him at Eighth and Chestnut Streets on Jeweler's Row, a huge jewelry store designed like a warehouse with several different venders. Toot and Micky knew that their loyalty was with Tone but, in the meantime, they had to make some money. Micky knew that his best shot at getting treated fairly in this messy game was for him to get with Champ, at least until Tone got back on his paper. Toot was down for whatever

Micky was down for. In fact, Micky had become their official spokesperson. Toot never verbally elected him but you could tell Micky called the shots.

"Damn, Micky, do you think your Uncle Champ will let you get in with him?"

"I don't know...but I'm going to try my hand."

"I hope he gets right at us because all of my niggas still be calling trying to get some work."

"Man, Toot, I lost count of how much money I could have made by now."

"Damn, as soon as we started getting that paper this dumb shit happens," Toot said in frustration.

"I know, my nigga, but we're going to be straight if I can get Champ to realize I'm a grown man and I'm trying to get at him on this paper tip."

"If Tone finds out he's going to be salty," Toot said.

"Tone won't find out," Micky interrupted, "but if he was to find out he couldn't be but so mad because he knows niggas got to eat."

When they pulled up to Eighth Street, they saw Champ's Bentley GTC parked outside. Micky double-parked down the street and told Toot to stay put. He knew Champ would never discuss business around anyone else. Toot wasn't sweating it; he just wanted to get put on.

When Micky entered the door, he noticed Wanna standing near Alex the Jeweler's showcase. It was no surprise that she would be standing there since Alex was by far the best jeweler in the row. Micky walked over to her.

"Hey, handsome," Wanna said, being caught off guard by his presence there.

"What's up, Aunt Wanna? What are you buying?" Micky asked, as if Wanna wasn't supposed to be there.

"Champ is buying me a ring," Wanna replied, with innocence.

"A ring?"

"Not an engagement ring, just a regular ring," Wanna said, startled by Micky's reaction.

"I know it wouldn't be an engagement ring, he is your god-brother," Micky replied, unaware that they had put the god-brother and god-sister shit to rest.

"Micky, we ain't on that brother and sister shit no more."

"Why not? What happened?"

"Nothing, we just started dating each other and now we're together," Wanna finally managed to say.

Before Micky could get another question out, Champ came from behind the counter with Alex.

"Alex, you remember little Ern?" Champ said, pointing at Micky.

"Yeah, I remember he was a little boy. He got big and he looks just like Ern," Alex said, shaking Micky's hand.

"Alex, I'll call you in two days. I need that ring by Thursday because we're going out of town on Friday," Champ said, leading Wanna and Micky out the door.

When they got outside, Wanna gave Micky a hug and a kiss on the cheek and went to sit in the car. Micky's little horny ass watched Wanna walk to Champs car the whole while thinking, *Aunt Wanna is a bad bitch.* He watched her ass switch across the street in her Yves Saint Laurent jeans. He was about to let his mind wander with thoughts of her until he felt Champ grab his shoulder.

"What's up, Nephew? What can I do for my favorite nephew?" Champ said, hoping he could help Micky. Champ loved Micky like a real nephew because Ern was like a real brother to him.

"Unc, this is some serious shit I want to holler at you about," Micky said, trying to find a way to put his words together.

"Ain't nothing that serious that you can't holler at your Uncle about it. What...you need some paper?" Champ said, pulling out a bankroll of hundred dollar bills.

"Naw, Unc, I don't need it like that," Micky said, pushing his hand over Champ's hand full of money, causing him to put it back in his pocket.

"Well, what's up? What, you got a bitch pregnant or do you have some drama? What is it, little nigga?" Champ said, sounding like Melvin from Baby Boy.

"Unc, I need some work," Micky said, now cutting through the bullshit.

"You can manage the restaurant, run the construction crews or you can be the property manager. Whatever you want to do, it's done," Champ said, thinking that Micky was talking about legit work.

"Naw, Unc...I need some of them bricks."

"Naw, Micky I can't do that. I'm not putting you in these streets. Ern would never approve of that," Champ said, with a look of disbelief on his face. He heard that Micky was hustling but he could never bring himself to believe it.

"Unc, I'm not little Micky anymore. Yes...I will be little Ern until the end of time but I'm a grown man. Furthermore, you're not putting me in the streets, I'm already in the streets. My connect is not around and, before I fuck with these crab-ass niggas, I figured I would come to family," Micky said, with a pleading tone.

"Micky these streets ain't sweet and, if you make any false moves, the streets will cost you your life. I can't do that to you. I got more than enough paper for us. You can get whatever, whenever," Champ said, pleading with his nephew.

"Unc, I know you're super good. You give me good money, you bought my first banshee, my first car, and you even rented that Maybach for my prom. Unc, you have done more than enough for me, but I need to get at and build my own shit. I'm telling you straight up that, with or without you, I'm getting in this game. I prefer that it be with you," Micky said, shooting his best shot at getting some work from Champ.

After a long, quiet pause, Champ looked Micky in the eyes.

"Nephew, let me give this shit some serious thought. I'm going to sleep on it tonight and I'll meet you at the breakfast store in the morning to let you know my answer," Champ said, giving Micky a handshake and a hug.

"Tell Aunt Wanna I said 'bye," said Micky.

Champ jumped into the Bentley with Wanna and Micky went back to his LS460.

Toot was impatient. He hardly let Micky put the car in drive before he started with the questions.

"What'd he say? Are we good? Do we have work now?"

"Slow down, Toot."

"Man, I just got two calls for some work while you were gone. I'm running out of stall-tactics."

"We're good, just relax, dawg," Micky said.

"So when are you going to get the work?"

"He said he'll think about it."

"Think about it?" Toot yelled.

"Yeah…at first he said flat out no. Then I told him that I was getting in the game with or without him. He then started thinking and asked me to let him sleep on it. He's gonna get with me tomorrow morning to let me know his answer. I know he's gonna let us eat because he normally answers yes or no and sticks to whatever it is he says, so for him to say that he would think about it means he is saying yes."

"So, basically, you're saying we're good, home-boy?" Toot said, smiling at the thought of making money again.

"Yeah, we're good, home-boy. It's me and you against the world."

~~~~~

Sab got the word that he could catch up with Boop at his aunt's house on 38th near Popular Street because Boop had been back and forth to her house to make sure she was good and to take her collected street money that was owed to Rocky. He, of course, pocketed some of the money. Sab was on point this time because he knew Boop wasn't sweet. He still didn't listen to Tone and bring his whole squad over to handle the work. Instead, it was just him and Dave.

They parked the car at the tip of 37th and Girard and got out to walk down the street. It wasn't hard to find out which house belonged to Rocky's mom. There was a crowd of family and friends going in and out of the house talking, drinking, and grieving together. Nobody paid any attention to the two strangers as they approached the house. They just assumed that they were supposed to be there. They saw Boop conversing with family members.

Boom, Boom, Boom!

Shots rang out and people started to scatter. Boop was hit in the leg. He ducked behind a water-ice stand and got his burner out. Sab and Dave moved closer and started emptying their clips at the water-ice stand. There were people screaming and crying at the sight of this Wild West shootout. Shy came out of nowhere and started busting his gun in the direction of Sab and Dave. Dave caught one in the head and dropped to the pavement. Sab, sensing shit would get hectic, started firing his Kel-Tec nonstop at Shy. He dropped Shy and hit a few innocent bystanders. He started jogging back to the car as Boop dragged himself to the middle of the street. Boop started busting the last of his bullets despite the fact he was badly hit.

All of a sudden, a black van began tearing down the street at 80 miles per hour and ran Boop over. Between his bullet wounds and the impact of the car, Boop didn't stand a chance. The van sped off, and Sab drove his car back to Camden without Dave.

"Damn, they killed my boy."

Chapter 9

Micky was up early watching the news with Toot at his apartment. Over the last week or so, Toot and Micky had gotten super close. They basically turned Micky's apartment into a club house. They never brought any bitches to the crib. Whenever they had time for bitches, amidst the running around for Tone, they always went to a hotel. When the newsman began to discuss last night's triple homicide, Toot turned up the volume.

"Good morning ladies and gentlemen. This is Walt Hunter and we are live in the Mantua section of West Philadelphia on 38th and Popular Streets. Last night, this was the scene of an urban blood bath that left three dead and four injured. The house behind me to my left, marked by the makeshift memorial of teddy bears and candles, is where the Pew family was already grieving the loss of their loved one, Ronald Pew. You may remember Pew, who was killed execution-style outside of his apartment along with his girlfriend, Tameeka James, two days ago when two gunmen allegedly walked up and opened fire on the couple. Sources close to the investigation say that one of the deceased here is believed to be one of those two gunmen. The Police Commissioner said they are conducting an ongoing investigation, but he is certain that the two murders are connected. He also suggested that this might be related to a drug war. We'll keep you posted as the investigation unfolds. I'm Walt Hunter, and this has been Channel 3 Eyewitness News."

Toot turned the volume down with a smile on his face.

"Nigga what are you smiling about?"

"Nigga you seen my work," Toot said, as if he shot people up.

Micky looked at Toot with a look of confusion and humor on his face.

"Nigga, what work? You ain't do shit," Micky said.

Toot sat back in his seat and looked at Micky as if he couldn't believe what he was hearing.

"Nigga, you heard that nigga, Boop...bones and everything breaking as I ran his bitch-ass over," Toot said.

"Whoop-dee-doo...you got a vehicular homicide on a nigga that was shot up," Micky said, laughing at Toot's work.

"Damn, baby-boy, you sound like your hatin' on my work," Toot said, as he joined in on the laughter.

"Naw, Toot, that was some wild shit," Micky said, picking up his car keys on his way to meet Champ.

"I hope your Uncle puts us on, my nigga," said Toot.

"We're good, I'm not letting him tell me no," Micky said, as he walked out the door.

When Micky got into the car, he popped in his Lil' Wayne and DJ Drama *Gangster Grillz* CD. He picked up the phone to call his mom as he drove to meet Champ. He always made sure to check on Sharon, who wasn't only his mom but his best friend. He felt good when his mom said she was cool and he felt even better about his chances of Champ putting him on because Champ called to make sure he would be on time. Micky was actually ten minutes early. When he got out of the car, he noticed

Champ pulling up and waited so they could go in together.

"What's up, Unc?" Micky said, shaking Champs hand.

"A little bit of me and a whole lot of you," Champ said, leading Micky into the store.

Rhonda led them to a booth in the back. Rhonda was mesmerized by Micky and his swagger. She knew they were around the same age and, when Champ introduced him as his nephew, she knew he was cut from a hell of a cloth. She took their orders and made mental notes about Micky's hygiene as she noticed his pearly-white teeth and manicured nails. They waited for her to place their order and get their drinks before they began to talk.

"Damn...when did she start working here?" Micky asked.

"A couple weeks ago, she's a rough little piece, ain't she?" Champ replied.

"Yeah, what's her story?"

"I don't know her like that. All I know is that she goes to Temple."

"I might have to sample that, but right now I'm trying to see what's up with you and me getting this money," Micky observed.

"Micky, I really don't want you in these streets," Champ told him.

"Unc, I'm already in and I told you with..."

"...Or without me, you're in," Champ said, cutting him off and completing his sentence.

"Unc, I'm a big boy. I got my father's blood running through me, and with you on my side I can make it," Micky said, being firm with Champ about his decision to get in the streets and on his paper.

"I think Ern would be upset if I let you in the game, but then again, he would be upset if I let you run around with a bunch or suckers instead of me showing you how to really get down. It's like I'm in a lose-lose situation."

"Unc, I think there's no other nigga in the world that my dad would want me to get down with besides you. My dad knows that, if I choose the game and you're there to guide me, I'd be straight. He knows that with you I'll be in this game full of funny shit without all the funny shit."

"Micky, if you want to get down...fuck it, you're down. You don't start at the bottom...you start at the top. What can you handle at 17,500 a brick?" Champ said, getting down to business.

"Unc, even if it's bullshit, I can do like 20 bricks a week, easy."

"Micky, you are dealing with the best of the best. You're my heart so I'll never fuck you or hustle you by giving you some bullshit. We got fish scale...straight fish scale, nephew."

"Damn, it's like that, Unc?"

"Yeah, it's like that," Champ said, as Rhonda walked up with their food. She put their food in front of them and asked if they needed anything else. Before she walked off she promised to come back to check on them again soon.

"So when can I start, Unc?" Micky asked as soon as he saw that Rhonda wasn't within earshot.

"You can start this evening. I'll bring you a car with a hydraulic stash box in it. I'll show you how to work it but I don't want you to show the box to nobody. Go buy a brand new prepaid and don't call anybody on it. I'll give you my direct line when I get to you. That phone will be just for me and you. Call your chicks and everybody else on your other phone. I still don't really talk on the prepaid; the most I'll say is that I'm coming to meet you. Last, but not least, don't let your mom find out that you're hustling and especially not for me, she would kill me," Champ instructed.

They ate the rest of their food discussing the crazy shit going down around Tone and how Micky was smarter than Tone. Micky paid for the meal.

"Keep the change and put this to use," Micky said, passing Rhonda 40 dollars and a napkin with his number on it.

"Sure will and you better answer," Rhonda said, blushing and glad that Micky made the first move.

Micky and Champ exchanged hugs and promised to catch up with each other later.

When Micky told Toot about how smoothly things went, Toot started calling his players and lining up sales. They were on their way to see Sab because he said he had a message for Tone. They met him in front of Palmers Night Club on Seventh and Spring Garden Streets. When Sab got out of the car, the sight of him made Micky and Toot look at each other. It has been 24 hours since they saw him last and he looked a mess. Sab hadn't slept since the shooting. Instead, he was getting high snorting coke and taking E-pills to absorb the pain of Dave's death. It hurt so bad because he and Dave had been friends since childhood.

"What's up, Sab?" Micky said.

"It ain't shit, little nigga."

"What do you want me to tell Tone?" Micky asked, wanting to get away from Sab who was super high and smelling like shit.

"Tell him I need about $50,000 so I can bury Dave and take care of something. Oh, and tell him I want to come see him."

"Sab, I'll tell him about the money and you'll be able to see him Friday. He comes home Thursday and he don't want you around the hospital because there's too much police activity around there," Micky said.

"Yeah, that's right. I'm going to kill that nigga's whole family because Dave was my brother."

"Okay, we'll get with you about that later."

"Okay...later," Sab said, staggering back to his car.

"Yo, that nigga is high as shit. He still had coke around his nose," Toot said, as they drove off.

"Yeah, that nigga smell like stone cold shit, too. Damn, that nigga smelled like a fucking dump truck!"

Toot started to laugh at Micky's comment.

"Damn, Tone got to get a fucking grip on, dude," Toot said, sipping on a Pepsi.

"Man, Tone need to get rid of that clown. We did all the work. Them niggas didn't do shit but draw on our situation. For real, we might have to fall back off Tone while we getting this money because his shit is going to be heated. I know the nigga is going to come home on some drawing shit and I just want to get this paper," Micky said, hoping Toot wouldn't be on no bullshit and ride with his cousin.

"I'm with you, Micky. I'm trying to get this money. Tone can have the bullshit! I want him to be okay, but he fucks with a bunch of clowns and their whole style is old school," Toot said.

Micky was glad he and Toot were on the same page.

"Tone already doesn't want us around the gunplay so we'll be able to fade right off of him. We'll just continue

to check on him every once in awhile. We'll go to the
hospital everyday to check on him, but once he's released
we're fading."

~~~~~

It was Monday night and every Monday in the city was
known as Magic Monday at Club Onyx. Magic Monday
originated in Atlanta, Georgia, at Magic City. Club Onyx
tried to offer Philly the same type of environment. It
wasn't as good as Magic City but it was as close as the
city got. Tonight, all the players were out and the dick-
eaters as well. Champ brought Wanna out with him and,
of course, he had his two favorite goons, Ducky and
Raheem, with him. Champ had the VIP booth with 10
bottles of Ace of Spades, two bottles of Patron, spring
waters, and some pineapple juice. On top of that, he had
$10,000 in one-dollar bills to play with throughout the
night.

Micky and Toot came in and made their way to
Champ's section.

"Damn, Unc, what's up?" Micky said.

Champ turned around and hugged Micky.

"What's up, Nephew, what's going on?" Champ asked,
sounding like a proud father.

"Ain't nothing. They hassled us at first until I told
them you were my uncle."

"Yeah, they are on some other shit at the door unless
you know somebody."

"Yo...you remember my little homie, Toot?" Micky
asked, neglecting to introduce Toot as Tone's cousin.

"Yeah, I see him with you a lot."

"Unc, this is my man."

"Well...he's my man too because I love what you love."

Champ reached out his hand and shook Toot's.

"Enjoy yourself, Toot, you're around family. That's Ducky and Raheem over there drinking up the champagne."

Toot shook their hands as Raheem passed him a bottle of Ace of Spades.

"Drink up, little nigga," Raheem said, deciding to make Toot comfortable since Champ said he was family.

"Get over here and show me some love, Little Micky," Ducky said, grabbing Micky by the head and hugging him.

"I'm not little no more, Ducky," Micky said, hugging Ducky back.

Ducky was like family to Micky and he would do anything for him, but he didn't fuck with Tone at all.

"You're always going to be Little Micky to me. I'm your big cousin."

Micky broke out of Ducky's bear hug to shake Raheem's hand.

"What's up, Raheem?"

"Nothing, little nigga. Get one of these bottles, we're balling tonight."

Before he could grab the bottle, he was in another bear hug, this time from Wanna.

"Hey, handsome."

"What's up, Aunt Wanna?" Micky said, hypnotized by her perfume.

"You behaving?"

"Yeah, I'm chilling."

"Leave him alone," Champ said, grabbing Wanna by the waist.

"I'm not messing with him...I just can't believe how grown he's getting."

"He's good," said Champ, "Let him enjoy himself. In fact, go get us a few chicks so I can get these little niggas some lap dances."

Wanna left to do as he instructed.

Champ wanted to discuss a little bit of business with Micky before things got wild.

"Micky, I wanted you to come out because I wanted you to know that this is our immediate circle, nobody else...just me, you, Raheem, and Ducky. Sure, you'll have customers and associates, but this is what we trust in, just us. We have lots of people in every part of this city, but this is our family. We got shooters if shit ever gets thick but, for the most part, this is our team."

"Can Toot be on the team?"

"Sure, but he's got to earn it by showing where his loyalty lies. If he don't let this paper come between y'all within the next year and you feel the same way by then...he's on the team. When there's a lot of money involved, everybody shows their true colors and, believe me, there's a lot of paper involved."

Just then Bingo walked up with Thelma, Teddy, Dawud, and Nino. Everybody exchanged handshakes and hugs. Champ was happy to see his cousin out having a good time with her husband. Ever since Champ stopped by the pool hall to have a talk with Bingo, he'd made a conscious decision to enjoy his life, his paper, and his wife.

"What's up, Cousin?" Thelma asked, hugging Champ.

Thelma loved Champ. He basically raised her. He looked out for her and always let it be known she was his heart.

"Nothing, Cousin, I'm happy to see you're smiling and that ring is crazy."

"Yeah, Cuz, I don't know what you told him, but he's been super good to me," Thelma whispered in his ear.

Wanna walked up with five girls.

"We need three more girls, Wanna," Champ said, waving his arms to let her know that more people had joined the party.

Before she could recognize anyone, Thelma grabbed her arm.

"What's up, Cousin?"

"What are you doing here, girl?" Wanna said, dragging Thelma along with her to get more girls.

The party was stepping up. Bingo ordered ten more bottles and got another ten thousand in ones to match Champs.

Micky was basically raised by all of these men. On any given day, these men would do anything for him. Ern looked out for each of them on some level when he was alive. It was said that Champ got his whole swagger from Ern. Micky was the last piece of Ern, and he was destined to show niggas that the apple didn't fall to far from the tree.

"Yo, get this chick right here, Micky," Teddy said, pulling Micky over to a Chinese girl.

Micky was getting a lap dance when Thelma and Wanna came back with the other chicks. The party was jumping. Bingo's crew was enjoying themselves with Champ's crew. The only bad blood from Ern, Champ, and Bingo's childhood crew was Tone.

"Look at Micky, he looks like Ern and y'all are turning him out," Thelma said, pointing at Micky who was getting a lap dance by a Puerto Rican chick by this time.

"Yeah, he does look like Ern," Wanna replied.

"What's up with you and my cousin? I heard y'all put that fake brother and sister shit to rest," Thelma said.

"Yeah, girl...now we are really cousins because Champ is mine and I'm here to stay."

"Do that, girl. As long as y'all are happy and he likes it, I love it."

Onyx was getting packed. All the hustlers in Philly were out and everybody was shining. Joe and Omar were out chilling with Omar's homie, Jabril. Belvin was repping Southwest and throwing stacks of money at the featured dancer on stage. Apple, Jig, and Omar Teggle were popping bottles and plotting on some bitches that had just walked through the door. Even Mustafa from Delaware decided to come out to enjoy himself with his crew. It was evident that the bitches would be out; they had a tendency to stalk the players. Bianca from Major Figures was out with her sister, Keisha, and their South Philly crew. Danielle and Tanya were at the bar getting drinks and scoping out the joint for the ballers. Brook and Sarena slid through to make an appearance, and Amanda, Kesha, and Aaliyah were sitting at a table sipping on a bottle that was sent over anonymously. Despite the various crews, everybody was there to enjoy themselves and there was no animosity.

Champ loved every bit of this shit. When the DJ played Young Jezzy's *Dope Boys Go Crazy* featuring Jay Z, the crowd became excited. Everyone in Champ's section stood on the edge of the VIP and made it rain ones from the $20,000 sitting on the table. There seemed to be an endless flow of money falling from the sky, which looked crazy because there was supposed to be a recession. The thirsty bitches were aware of where the money was coming from and they were eager to get at it. With Wanna and Thelma on deck, the bitches could forget about sucking Champ or Bingo's dicks, but the rest of the squad was fair game. To Micky's surprise, Rhonda walked up and hugged him.

"What are you doing here?" Micky said.

"The same thing you're doing here. I called you and you didn't answer, so I let my friends drag me out."

"My phone died but I'm glad you're here so I can have someone to hang with."

"Oh, I can hang with the bosses tonight?" Rhonda asked, sarcastically.

"Sure you can. Go get your girls and chill with us."

She left and came back with two girlfriends and Micky and his crew showed them the time of their lives. The night went smoothly and the let out was crazy. The niggas had their wheels out and some of the bitches were stunting as well. The front of the building was packed with Bentleys, Maseratis, Aston Martins, Ranges, and a few Benzes. Ducky and Raheem made sure to follow Champ's crew off the lot while Dawud and Nino took care of Bingo's crew.

Chapter 10

It had been weeks since Tone had seen the streets. Things had changed for everybody during that time, including him. Whether he knew it or not, the streets didn't stop when a player got popped. He had lost a tremendous amount of power on the street. His number one young bull, Bam, was dead. Bam was not only a big part of Tone's muscle, but he also pushed a lot of Tone's bullshit coke off on a lot of niggas.

Tone had a lot of new enemies, some he knew of and others he didn't. Sab was even beginning to convince himself that Tone was the reason for Dave's death. Sharon loved Tone to death, but his being away allotted her time to reconsider their relationship and how bad it looked to the public. She was slowly but surely beginning to put their relationship to rest. His best bet on salvaging his empire was through Micky and Toot, but he was too naïve to recognize what he had before him in the two up-and-coming hustlers. Besides, with the way Champ was treating them, Tone's dawg ass was sure to lose them.

Normally, when a hustler of this magnitude is released from jail or the hospital, there are a whole lot of people around waiting for their reappearance. The only people that were waiting for Tone were his mom, Sharon, Toot, Micky, and Wanna. Wanna was there solely to support

Sharon; her concern for Tone was only out of respect for her girlfriend.

"Sharon, I know you're glad your man is coming home today."

"Wanna, I just hope he comes home and sits his old ass down. There's too much going on the streets."

"I'm with you on that one, girl."

"I almost lost my life and the life of my son fucking around when them hatin' ass niggas came and killed Ern."

"I know that was crazy, Sharon. People don't give a fuck no more."

"Yeah, look how Meeka got killed fucking with that young bull Rocky. They killed them in broad daylight."

"Yeah, Sharon, you know I didn't care for Meeka but I don't wish death on nobody," Wanna said, looking at the floor not wanting to see the hurt in Sharon's eyes.

No matter how much Wanna used to warn Sharon about Meeka's shadiness, Wanna knew that Sharon had a soft spot for Meeka.

"Yeah they did her dirt, girl...that's a shame. Her funeral is Saturday."

"Are you going?"

"Naw, I'm not going to the funeral, but I'm going to the viewing just to pay my respects. Will you go with me?" Sharon asked her.

Wanna looked up at Sharon shaking her head.

"Sharon, you know I didn't get down like that with that girl." She paused for a moment and briefly placed her hands over her face before she continued, "If it will make you happy I'll go to the viewing with you...but just the viewing."

"Okay, girl, and you don't have to repeat just the viewing like that," Sharon said, mugging her girlfriend in a playful manner.

Micky and Toot walked over to where the ladies were standing.

"What's up, Mom and Aunt Wanna?"

"What's up, nothing...you better come give your mother a hug," Sharon said, with her arms stretched out to hug her only child.

Micky hugged his mother then leaned in to give his aunt one. Toot spoke and waved to the ladies then went over to holler at his Aunt Bernadette.

"What are you planning to do today, son?" asked Sharon.

"I'm going to be busy, why Mom?"

"Because I was going to cook dinner and I wanted you to come by and get something to eat."

"Mom, I'm supposed to go out to dinner with my friend."

"What friend?"

Micky was hesitant to answer.

"Some chick I'm dating."

"Dating? Oh, so you got a girlfriend and I haven't met her?"

"She's not my girl, Mom, we're just friends."

Sharon smiled at her son before she continued.

"Well...any friend of my son is a friend of mine, and I think you should bring her to dinner tonight so I can meet her."

Micky paused considering the proposal.

"Okay, Mom...but remember I'm 18-years-old, so don't be trying to play me in front of her."

"Play you?" Sharon asked, innocently, "Ain't nobody going to play your big-head self," she replied, now mugging Micky the way she did Wanna earlier.

Micky pointed his finger at her in the same manner she used to when she scolded him as a child.

"Mom, I'm a player now, so when I come over don't be pinching me on the cheek and all that stuff."

"Boy, I'll pinch you whenever I want," Sharon said, as she pinched his cheek.

Wanna stood close by watching and admiring the relationship Sharon had with her son.

~~~~~

The doctor came out into the lobby followed by Tone. Tone was happy to see that everyone was there waiting.

"Mr. Davis, get plenty of rest and don't do anything that requires lifting and pulling."

"Okay, Doc," Tone said, while thinking, *Fuck you, Doc.*

"Take your medication as prescribed to prevent infections."

"Okay, Doc."

The doctor walked off leaving Tone, who was free to leave, with his family.

"I love y'all and thanks for coming to see me, but I'm ready to get to the crib. Come up to the house tonight so I can see everybody," Tone said, as he gave everyone a hug and a handshake before heading to the door. Sharon and Bernadette rode with Tone while the others went their separate ways. Wanna went to meet Champ for lunch while Micky and Toot went to handle their business.

~~~~~

Teddy was making his way up the ladder. With Bingo preparing to retire, Teddy knew that he would be next in line to run the business. Teddy loved his older brother but their styles were totally different. Bingo was laid back and gave niggas a chance to right any wrongs that they may have done to him. Many people took his kindness for weakness, but trusted and believed there was nothing weak about Bingo.

One time, this nigga, Mark, who grew up with Bingo, asked him for a brick on consignment. Bingo fronted him the brick at $19,000. Two days later, Mark came to Bingo with a sob story about how someone broke into his spot and stole everything. Bingo wasn't tripping. He basically told Mark to get the money back to him when he could. Teddy was mad when he caught wind of the story and asked Bingo for permission to handle Mark. Bingo's theory was that if it only took $19,000 for Mark not to be able to come around again then it was money well spent. Teddy wasn't feeling Bingo's logic. He thought his brother was getting soft, until one day Bingo told Teddy to take a ride with him. Teddy went with Bingo to one of the properties he had on 38th Street and Haverford Avenue. Teddy didn't realize what was going on until he went down into the basement. Mark was chained to a chair with duck tape across his mouth and upper body. Teddy could tell Mark had been pistol whipped by the bumps and bruises apparent on his face. Teddy wasn't prepared for what happened next. Bingo pulled out his .40 Cal and put his silencer on it before he emptied two shots into Mark's head. He then took out a straight blade and cut out Mark's tongue. Teddy had never seen Bingo this way and all he could think about was his statement about the $19,000 being a "well spent" loss. He immediately questioned his brother about his change of heart. Bingo assured Teddy that it wasn't about the money, that he could care less about the money.

"Nigga, I ain't worried about that punk-ass 19," Bingo explained, "That's broad money, nigga. Shit, I can spend that at a bar! That nigga went around the city saying that he took something from me...that's why I had to cut his tongue out."

They wrapped Mark's body in a blanket, put him in Bingo's work van, and left him in the park. Teddy had a new respect for Bingo, but he still felt that he wouldn't let the nigga, Mark, have a pass in the first place. He had plans on running things differently once he was in charge.

Teddy knew Bingo would downplay the Tone shit on some old-school policy, so he decided to keep his plans for Tone on the down-low between Dawud and Nino. He was not about to let Tone's disrespect slide.

"Yo, man, as soon as this faggot nigga, Tone, gets back in these streets we're airing the nigga back out," Teddy said, eating a mushroom chicken cheese steak.

"Yeah, but we ain't putting rookie shit down like Rocky and them did. I'm going to give that nigga a face lift with my A-R," Nino said, picking up his gun.

"Damn, nigga, you're fucking that steak up," Dawud chimed in.

"Nigga, you know how Max's steaks are...sloppy and good as a motherfucker," Teddy said, wiping his face with a napkin.

"They ain't that mother-fucking good!"

"Dawud, I think your greedy ass wants some. Take a piece," Teddy said, holding out half of his sandwich.

Dawud, being the greedy nigga that he was, reached for the steak. Teddy smacked his hand away with his free hand.

"Get the fuck outta here, nigga. Order your own," Teddy said, as Nino burst out laughing.

"Teddy you're a fucking nut and what the fuck is so funny, Nino?" Dawud spat, now mad at both of his friends.

They all really loved each other and joked around with each other like this all the time. At times, they became upset with one another, but they would never wrong each other.

"Naw, Dawud, you can have that half right there," Teddy said, pointing at the half steak instead of lifting it up this time.

Dawud's greedy ass picked up the steak and went to work on it.

"You're eating that steak like it's your last one," Nino said.

"Man, this motherfucker is banging," Dawud said, between chews.

"Yo, anyway...let's get back to this nigga, Tone. I want that nigga out of here."

"Say no more," Dawud said, woofing down the remainder of the steak.

"Man, Micky is going to be fucked up about his step-pop," Nino observed.

"Micky will be okay and he'll never know it came from us. You know that Micky is my little man," Teddy said.

"Yeah...shorty is thorough," Dawud said, looking around like he wanted another cheese steak.

"Besides, it's time for Tone to go. Everyone from his era was dead, in jail, or about to pass the power down. Like Champ and Bingo. They're from his era, but they fall back and aren't competing with the up-and-coming niggas. I bet if Tone was out with us at Onyx on Monday he would have had us in some competing shit with other niggas," Teddy said, thinking about how much shit Teddy used to have Bingo involved in.

"I don't like the fact that he had the balls to come in my brother's place of business and question him. That's the shit I be telling Bingo about, that passive shit. Plus, I be hearing his name in the middle of Ern's death too much. Ern was my fucking old-head. Hands down, feet up, he was the smoothest nigga in our city," Teddy said, and Dawud and Nino had to agree. They didn't have the same rapport with Ern as Teddy, but they knew him and he always showed love to the young bulls.

"Do you remember when All Star weekend was in Philly and the niggas thought they were stunting outside the party that A.I. had at the Gallery?' Teddy asked them, "Niggas didn't know that Ern went and copped that crazy whip. When he pulled up in that cream Bentley Azure with those 24s on it and hopped out, the game was over. Bingo and Champ ran over to their boy and bigged him up, not on no dick-eating shit, but they were basically saying, 'Y'all niggas, see how our boy is doing it'," Teddy said.

"Yeah, you remember Tone's hatin' ass stayed across the street talking to Chanel and Raquil with a salty look on his face," Dawud said, causing Teddy to think back a little harder.

"Damn, I can see that nigga's face like it was yesterday. That nigga was really hatin' on my old-head and that was supposed to be his boy," Teddy said.

"Fuck it, I'm putting an extra slug in his face for Ern," Dawud promised.

"Yo, let's play some Madden," Nino said, getting tired of talking about Tone's slimy ass.

"I'll bust your ass first, but why are you changing the subject?" Teddy said, as he grabbed the joystick.

"Because you done called the shot and we're gonna kill that grimy motherfucker," Nino said, as he turned the game on.

"I got winners," Dawud shouted out.

"Your game is the weakest, Dawud," Teddy said, as Nino started laughing again.

"I see y'all are on some Beavis and Butt-head shit today. Teddy tells all the whack-ass jokes and Nino, a.k.a. Butt-head, just cracks up laughing," Dawud remarked.

They all laughed at Dawud's last comment.

"You seem to have all the jokes, Dawud," Nino said, winning the coin toss on Madden.

They stayed at the tire shop all day, everyday, unless one of them got called for business or by a chick to come kick it.

~~~~~

Tone was happy to be home. It was a big relief to be at the crib eating real food. Of course, he fucked the shit out of Sharon when they got to the house. He sent Ms. Bernadette to the supermarket to buy groceries that they already had in the house so he could get a quickie. With her gone, the only one that could hear them fucking was Cavalli. By the time Bernadette got back, they were finished. It was times like this that Sharon's mind got clouded and she felt as though she belonged with Tone. Nobody had ever dicked her down like Tone and she was sprung over his game. Even with one arm, Tone was throwing his back into it, which made Sharon wish that Ms. Bernadette wasn't coming back at all and that she hadn't invited Micky over for dinner. She knew it was too late to call it off, so she got up to help Ms. Bernadette cook.

Tone was on the phone with a few of his people trying to get everything lined up so he could get back at his paper and get at Teddy and his crew. He even made plans to get at Champ if the opportunity presented itself. A lot of people had changed their numbers on Tone and he was pissed off about that. In his sick mind, they all crossed him by doing so. He talked to Sab and planned to meet him in the morning. Sab was begging for money over the phone and Tone could tell he was either high or drunk by the way he was slurring his words.

I'm going to have to kill this nigga, too, after I get him to help me get rid of the last bit of niggas, because he knows too many of my secrets, Tone thought.

Tone was snatched out of his daydream by the doorbell ringing.

"Who the fuck is at our door," Tone said aloud, as he jogged down the steps.

Sharon had already opened the door for Micky and Rhonda as they walked into the house. Rhonda wore a pair of Rock and Republic jeans and shirt with open-toed Gucci sandals that showed her well-manicured feet.

"Mom, this is my friend, Rhonda," Micky said.

"How are you doing, Rhonda? My name is Sharon. It's nice to meet you."

"It's nice to meet you, too, Ms. Sharon," Rhonda replied.

"Just call me Sharon. The Miss thing makes me feel old."

"You don't look old. You could actually pass as Micky's sister."

"Oh, child, I like you already," Sharon said, smiling at the compliment.

Rhonda wasn't lying or just saying that to make Sharon feel good. Sharon looked real good for her age and her body was tight.

"Come Rhonda, let me introduce you to my man and his mom," Sharon said, as she walked away with Cavalli trailing behind her.

"This is my man, Tone," Sharon told her.

Rhonda shook Tone's hand looking like she seen a ghost. She couldn't believe that Micky's mom was with this clown.

"Hi Rhonda," Tone said, undressing her with his eyes and holding her hand too tightly as he shook it.

Rhonda felt disgusted. Sharon grabbed her hand and led her into the kitchen to meet Ms. Bernadette leaving the two men together.

"Damn, little, nigga...you scored one right there. She is a star," Tone said, as if he was proud of Micky but deep down hating the fact that Micky had pulled Rhonda when he couldn't.

"Yeah, that's a little something, Tone."

"Where you pull that from, my nigga?" Tone said, to see if Micky would lie.

"I pulled her out of Uncle Champ's breakfast store. She works there," Micky said.

Tone was jealous of Champ and hated when Micky addressed him as Uncle.

"Yeah, dude keep some freaks and cum dogs working up in there," Tone said, trying to get Micky to second-guess Rhonda.

"Yeah, he do, but she's not one of them. She works there part time because she goes to college down the street from the breakfast store. I went and met her parents. She comes from money, so she's not thirsty, main man. They got a big ass single home in Bucks County. Basically she has all the qualities of a keeper," Micky said, as smoothly as Ern would have, basically shutting down all the hating shit Tone was spitting. Tone was so salty he decided he wasn't going to let Micky know until a month after he started selling bricks again that he had coke.

Sharon and Ms Bernadette were enjoying Rhonda's conversation and company. Even Cavalli was feeling Rhonda because she was chilling in Rhonda's lap, which was weird because Cavalli didn't like strangers. After awhile, Tone settled down and chilled out. But he still occasionally undressed Rhonda with his eyes, which freaked the fuck out of her. She decided against telling Micky because she didn't want to cause any friction.

Overall, it was a good night. Rhonda enjoyed herself with Ms. Bernadette and Sharon and they enjoyed their time spent with her. Rhonda and Sharon even made plans to go shopping. Micky and Rhonda said their good-byes and were on their way out the door when Sharon whispered in his ear, "She's a keeper, Micky."

Micky flashed his million-dollar smile and hit the highway back to Philly planning his take over with Champ and his escape from hatin' ass Tone.

Chapter 11

Weeks went by and Tone was losing his cool. He had become so self-conscious about his dead arm, he kept thinking everyone was looking at it when, in reality, people weren't paying his arm no damn mind. He became bitter with life itself, and because of that, he attempted to make everybody else miserable.

Everybody began to distance themselves from Tone and he noticed it. The only person who stayed around him day in and day out was Sab. Initially, Tone would be with Sab to get at the few niggas he had on his list. After they rode around putting their murder plans into effect, they would sit in this little hole-in-the-wall bar on 27th and Indiana Streets named Double Down to get wasted. Tone tried to get Sab to stop snorting coke but was unsuccessful. Sab needed the coke to deal with the harsh reality of Dave being killed right in front of him.

One day, Sab was able to convince Tone to try the powder and, to Tone's surprise, it made him feel good. He didn't even stress about his dead arm while he was high. The powder made him feel like Tony Montana. As a result, he would bust his gun unconsciously when he went to put in work with Sab. Above all, it made him fuck like a wild horse.

Tone was unaware of the fact that his entire empire was falling apart due to his jealousy and his new habit. He was so focused on revenge that he barely hustled. He would only serve the niggas from Camden through Sab. In his mind, the whole of Philly was at war with him aside from Toot and Micky, but even they were suspect. Little did he know, Toot and Micky were on the rise and had no intention of fucking with his silly ass. The fact that they were distancing themselves from Tone was unnoticeable because they made sure to keep checking with him as planned. Tone felt he was being spiteful by not giving Micky and Toot any work. He kept telling them that he was going to get at them once he finished cleaning up the streets. It was a good thing Champ had them eating because they would have starved waiting for Tone.

Tone was up early, but he stayed in the house until noon because he had to go to the hospital for an evaluation before he picked up Sab. Sharon came home from the clinic. She walked pass Tone and went straight to the bedroom without saying a word.

"What's up with this retarded bitch walking by a player like she didn't see me?" Tone said quietly to himself, as his bitterness kicked in.

"Hi to you, too, you dusty bitch!" Tone yelled out loudly.

Sharon came to the bottom of the stairs to make sure she heard him correctly.

"What did you say?"

"I said...Hi to you, too, you dusty bitch. Walking in my house and not acknowledging a fucking player."

Sharon sighed to herself. She was appalled by Tone's arrogance and lack of memory so she decided to clear the air.

"First of all, this is *our* house. I paid just as much as you did. Second of all, when I see a player I'll acknowledge him. And lastly, I've never been dusty nor have I've ever been anybody's bitch, you fucking bastard."

"Bitch, you'll be whatever the fuck I call you. If you don't watch your mouth I'll smack the shit out of you," Tone retorted.

"Pussy, I just came from the clinic and they said I have gonorrhea. You want me to acknowledge you, nigga? Fuck you!" Sharon said, out of character because she was mad about having her first STD.

"I ain't give that shit to you," Tone said, knowing damn well his dick's been burning like hell when he pees.

Sharon stepped back to re-gain her composure.

"Tone, I don't even speak to other niggas let alone sleep with them," Sharon said, now killing Tone with kindness, "So go get your dirty dick checked out and use a condom when you fuck your little bitches."

"You must have gotten it from one of them little niggas you was fucking while I was in the hospital," Tone said.

Sharon was crushed. She couldn't believe Tone would burn her and play with her intelligence, but on top of that he had the nerve to accuse her of fucking around.

"I hate you! Pussy! I was at that hospital everyday making sure your dumb ass didn't die...you dead-arm pussy!"

CRACK!

Tone smacked the shit out of Sharon with his good arm causing her to fall. Before she could get up, he was choking her.

"You little, ungrateful bitch! If it wasn't for me you and your little punk-ass son would be out on the streets. If you ever talk to me like that again I'll kill you," Tone said, with the look of the devil in his eyes.

Sharon kicked Tone in the balls and he stumbled backwards. Sharon ran upstairs and locked herself in the bedroom.

This pussy must have lost his fucking mind putting his hands on me, she thought with shock. *What the fuck did he mean me and Micky would have been on the streets? He got the game fucked up. Ern made sure me and my son were straight. This is my fault for fucking with this nigga.*

Boom, Boom!

"Open this door bitch before I break it down," Tone shouted through the door, as he pounded on it.

"Tone, I'm on the phone with the cops and they're on their way right now," Sharon yelled back.

"Yeah, his name is Anthony Davis," Sharon said, loud enough for Tone to hear and knowing damn well he didn't fuck with the cops. She would never have really called the cops, not even on her worst enemy, but she knew the thought of them coming would make Tone leave the house. It worked, because Tone ran out of the house, jumped into his Benz, and drove away.

Tone drove down the expressway toward Philly mad as shit. He was in desperate need of a snort of coke. *Damn, I can't believe that bitch called the cops on me,* he thought, *All I ever did was look out for the bitch and her son. I got to find out which one of them bitches burned me, and when I do, I'm going to kill that bitch for putting these nuts on fire.*"

Tone's conversation with himself was interrupted when his phone rang. He looked at the caller ID and saw it was Micky. He contemplated not answering the phone thinking Sharon must have called him about their drama.

"Hello," Tone answered, expecting Micky to talk shit about him hitting Sharon.

"What's up O.G.?" Micky said, on the other end of the phone.

"It ain't shit, I'm on my way to the hospital."

"To the hospital, what's wrong?"

"I'm going to get this stupid arm evaluated," Tone said, pulling off the Broad Street exit.

"I was just calling to check on you, my nigga," said Micky.

"I'm good. I'll hit you later," Tone told him.

"That's what's up...one," Micky said, and hung up.

Tone pulled into the parking lot and went into the hospital for his appointment.

Sharon cleaned herself up and went to meet Wanna. They went to have drinks and lunch at John's on South Street. Although Sharon's face wasn't bruised from the smack her nose bled, but she was able to clean it up. The only mark she had was from Tone hurting her feelings and no one could see that mark because it was on her heart. No man had ever put his hands on her before today, and she vowed he would be the last one to ever do so.

Wanna could tell there was something wrong with Sharon because she seemed out of it.

"What's up, girl? You seem like you're on another planet."

"Oh, girl, I just got a lot on my mind," Sharon said, partially lying to her best friend.

"What did that nigga, Tone, do now?" Wanna asked, knowing he did something because Sharon had been calling her with bullshit about Tone for the past few days.

Sharon informed her of everything; his not coming home, their arguing, his slacking on hygiene, and the bitches that called to play on her phone.

Wanna knew Tone was putting Sharon through a lot, but she wasn't prepared for what happened next.

Sharon broke into tears in the middle of the restaurant. She was crying so hard Wanna had to tell the waiter to excuse them for a moment. Wanna was patient by nature, so she waited for Sharon to get her tears and emotions out before she said anything.

"Sharon, I haven't seen you cry since Ern's funeral. What's wrong, girl?" Wanna said, in a comforting tone to assure her girlfriend that she had her back.

"Wanna, this is between me and you, okay?" Sharon said, letting Wanna know that it was serious.

"Girl, I've never told a soul any of your secrets," Wanna said, honestly.

Wanna was loyal to Sharon and she always had her best interest at heart.

"That stinking bastard smacked and choked me today." Sharon confided.

Although Wanna was light brown, she managed to turn red in the face after hearing that Tone hit her friend.

"Where is that no good motherfucker at?" Wanna said, out of character due to her anger.

"I don't know. You can't tell anybody because I don't want anybody to get in trouble over that sad-ass motherfucker."

"You should tell Champ," Wanna said, knowing that even with two arms, Tone couldn't beat Champ.

"No, no, no...don't tell Champ. I don't want Champ getting into it with him and I damn sure don't want him telling Micky."

"Somebody's got to punch that weirdo in the mouth. I can't believe he fucking hit you! What are you going to do?"

"Wanna, I'm leaving that motherfucker as soon as I work out my exit plan."

"Exit plan? You don't need no exit plan! Just pack your shit and leave. I'll go with you now, and I dare him to come trippin' because I got my shit right in the car," Wanna said, seriously.

Wanna was licensed to carry the 380 pistol that she kept in her car, and over Sharon...she just might use it.

"I got this, girl. Please let me handle this," Sharon pleaded.

"Sharon, you know I don't get into your relationship and I've never voiced my opinion on you being with that snake, but I'll voice my opinion on your leaving him. Leave that sorry motherfucker!" Wanna said, with conviction in her voice.

"The crazy thing is that he hit me because I was mad he gave me gonorrhea. Now ain't that some shit?"

"Ooww, I hate that one-arm bastard," Wanna said.

"I hate him, too, girl. I've never had an STD in my life!"

"I'm going to let you work on your exit plan, but if you don't look like you're exiting I'm telling Champ and Micky. Deal?"

"Deal. Now where is that damn waiter with his fine ass," Sharon said, in need of a drink and wanting to change the subject.

"There he goes. Over here, handsome," Wanna said, as she flagged the waiter down.

The waiter came to the table after he placed the drinks on the one he was standing near.

"Hey, Ladies, I'm Michael, and I'll be waiting on y'all. Can I get y'all something to drink while you look over the menu?"

"Yeah, you can get us something to drink and you can take our order now," Sharon said, speaking for both of them.

"What will you ladies have today?"

"We'll have the buffalo shrimp Caesar salad and two apple martinis," Wanna answered.

When the waiter left, Wanna excused herself to use the restroom. Sharon used the time to call Tone who answered on the second ring.

"Hello," Tone said, trying to act like he had an attitude.

"What did the doctor say?"

"I didn't go to the doctor's," Tone said, thinking she was referring to getting his dick checked.

"So you didn't go to your evaluation?"

"Oh yeah, I thought you were talking about that other thing," Tone said, feeling like a nut.

"What did he say?"

"He said that I'm cool," Tone said, knowing they were talking about that amputation shit.

"Well...I was just checking on you."

"Sharon, I didn't mean to hit you. I'm sorry, okay, boo?"

"Yeah, Tone, I'm sorry for talking back to you and being mean."

"What did you tell the cops?"

"I didn't even call them. I would never call the cops on my Pretty Tony," Sharon said, working her charm on him.

"I knew you wouldn't do that shit to me. But, for real, boo...you had me bitching like a motherfucker," Tone said, relieved that he wasn't on the run from the cops.

"I'll see you when you get home, okay, Tony?"

"Okay, boo...I love you."

"I love you, too," Sharon said, as she hung up.

Wanna came back just before the waiter brought their food. They discussed their life-long friendship over their meal.

"Girl, I can say this without a second thought. You always have my back and you never gave up on getting that nigga, Champ," Sharon said.

"Sharon, you're my girl...my sister and I love you without limits. I'm going to love you no matter the conditions or consequences. As far as Champ goes, I'm glad that I pursued him because I don't know another chick that deserves him. He's a real man and he wears this pussy out."

The girls laughed and high-fived.

"I love how he always made sure that me and Micky were okay even though he knew Ern left us more than enough money. Champ is genuine and I wish y'all the best."

"Thanks, girl, but that's just him. He makes sure everybody is straight, especially the ones he loves. Micky is his heart."

"Did you know that Micky wants to trade his Lexus in and wants me to co-sign for a Maserati?" Sharon asked, shaking her head.

"Well...I guess he'll be getting a Maserati."

"I don't know Wanna. He's only 18-years-old and people know he's Ern's son. I don't want people thinking he has more than he really has and hurt my baby."

"I see your point, Sharon, but people think that we all have Rockefeller money anyway."

"You got a point there," Sharon replied. "I told him I would think about it."

"What's up with Rhonda? She hasn't come out with us in awhile."

"She has finals," Sharon told her. "She said that she left you a message last night."

"Champ was working me out and I left my cell downstairs."

"You are nasty."

"And you know it, girl," Wanna said, laughing.

"I love Rhonda for Micky. She is a good, young girl and the best new friend we ever had," Sharon explained.

"Yeah, that's my girl and she loves the mall as much as we do," Wanna added.

"She called you last night to thank you for that YSL bag and belt that you damn near fought her to accept as a gift from us."

"Sharon, that belt and bag was cold and it was so her. Plus, Micky put her up under two of the flyest bitches in Philly so she got to keep some cold pieces."

They declined dessert, paid the check, and left the restaurant feeling better. That's what they did for each other their whole lives - made each other feel like they were good as long as the other was a phone call away.

~~~~~

Teddy and Nino were chilling in the tire shop playing Madden and waiting for Dawud to come back from making a run. They had plans to go to Scooters Pub at 38th and Lancaster to have a few drinks and fuck with the bitches that came through during happy hour.

"I should've gone with that nigga. He done turned off his cell phone now. He must be fucking with his baby-mom or something," Teddy said to Nino, who was beating the shit out of him in Madden.

"He'll be here soon. That nigga definitely wants to go down Scooters and eat a hun-nit wings."

"It's a hundred not a hun-nit."

"Man, that nigga don't eat proper so I don't have to say it proper. He eat a hun-nit and you need to start this game over before I score a hun-nit on you," Nino said, laughing.

Teddy had to laugh, too. Just when Teddy was about to call Dawud again, his phone rang.

"Yo, what's up, Ducky? What it do?" Teddy said, into the receiver.

"It ain't shit...I just pulled up on the corner of Wallace Street at the Chinese store and the cops are everywhere."

"So, what that got to do with me?" Teddy asked, confused as to why Ducky would think he cared.

"It's a body in the middle of the street with a white sheet over it and people are saying that it's Dawud," Ducky said, sad to have to be the one to give Teddy the bad news.

The phone went dead. Teddy hung up without saying another word to Ducky. He couldn't believe what he was hearing.

"Yo, Nino, they said Dawud is in the street."

Teddy's face went blank.

"What the fuck is he doing in the street?"

"He got shot. He's on Wallace Street. Put your gun up...we got to get down 38th Street."

Nino put his burner behind the counter and they were out.

When they got to Wallace Street, everybody was out and cops were everywhere. As usual, nobody talked to the police. Just like in every other hood, the news traveled fast.

Dawud's mom was running up and trying to get behind the yellow tape but was stopped by a cop.

"Ma'am, you can't come pass this tape."

"They said that's my baby under there."

The cop waved over to the detective.

Detective Hutson came over and was informed the lady was the victim's mother. He lifted the tape and said, "Ma'am, come with me to identify the body."

"Okay, people, there's nothing to see here. If you have any information please come down to the station," Detective Starks said, trying to diffuse the crowd.

Nobody moved. They paid him no mind. Teddy couldn't believe that his boy was in the middle of the street dead. Although nobody talked to the cops, they were all talking to each other.

"Teddy, let me holler at you," Ducky said.

"What's up, Ducky?" Teddy asked, as they walked to a more secluded spot.

"Yo, Dawud was my man, too. If you need me, just call and I'll ride," Ducky said, as he gave Teddy a hug.

"Ducky, this shit is crazy. He just left me and this shit happened."

"Teddy, I stuck around to let you know that I'm a phone call away for whatever against whoever. Yo...holler at this young bull right here," Ducky said, holding little Woody.

He walked off into the crowd and got into his car.

"What's up, young bull?" Teddy said to Woody.

"What's up, old-head?" Woody replied.

"Did you see what happened?"

"Yeah, Dawud had just ordered some chicken and then this cross-eyed dude came up with a burner and started blasting. He stood over Dawud and hit him some more until this black Maxima pulled up and he jumped into the passenger side and rolled out," the young bull said, looking around to make sure nobody heard him running his mouth about the murder.

"How do you know the dude was cross-eyed?" asked Teddy.

"Because it looked like he was looking at me when he pulled the burner out, but when he shot you could tell he was looking at Dawud."

"Thanks, little nigga," Teddy said.

Teddy got Nino and they were out with nothing but murder on their minds. They silently vowed to never rest until the nigga that did that to Dawud was dead.

Chapter 12

Champ was impressed by Micky's movement. With Micky moving so smoothly and so much, Champ was able to spend more time planning his retirement. It also allowed him to spend more time with Wanna to build their empire and their relationship.

He was falling head over heels for Wanna who had already fallen hard for him. They were so compatible. Champ was beginning to realize just how much Wanna had his back. It seemed as if her whole world revolved around him and it seemed as if it had been like that forever. Now that they were a couple, it seemed as if she actually desired to do whatever he needed her to do to make him happy. Wanna was a jewel, and the only regret Champ had was that he hadn't realized it sooner. He couldn't get enough of her. She had her own paper, she was smart, the pussy was to the moon, and the dick suck was out of this world.

Champ was up early because he was supposed to meet Ducky and Micky at Champions. He was in the bathroom brushing his teeth with nothing on but his boxer briefs. Wanna walked in on him and caught him flexing in the mirror.

"What are you up so early for?" Wanna asked.

"I got to go make the turkey bacon, baby."

Wanna laughed at the reference before responding.

"We got enough turkey bacon to last a lifetime, Champ."

"Well...we can work on our second life," Champ said, smiling and knowing damn well he was working on getting out the game.

"What-ever," Wanna said, in a mock voice to sound like a character in the movie *White Chicks*.

She looked down and paused for a moment.

"Champ, what's that?" she asked, pointing at his drawers.

"Oh, that's my pool stick," Champ said, with a smirk.

Wanna moved in closer.

"Well...let me chalk it up," she said, grabbing his dick.

Champ stepped back and said, "No, baby, I have a meeting with..."

Champ couldn't complete his sentence. Wanna pulled his dick out of his drawers and started licking the head with long, slow tongue strokes. Champ was up against the sink breathing heavily. His toes curled. Wanna shoved as much of his dick in her mouth as she could. The slowness of her stroke combined with the wetness of her mouth made Champ's dick stiff. As she glided her warm mouth up and down his shaft, Champ began to lose control and had to hold onto the edge of the sink for support. His grunts and groans excited Wanna, and her pussy began to moisten soaking through the sheer panties that barely covered her ass. Wanna could feel Champ's excitement and decided to pull back.

"I'm done," she said, as she looked up at Champ, who was stunned by how abruptly she stopped.

"Sorry to hear that," Champ said, as he wrapped one hand into her hair and pushed her head back down on his dick.

That made Wanna even more excited and she began to suck his dick faster and harder. Champ put his remaining hand on her titty and began to fondle her nipple. He knew how turned-on she would be by that. The sensation from her nipples made Wanna even more aggressive. The way she curled her tongue around his dick made her spit slide down over Champ's balls.

"Damn, Wanna, I'm cumming," Champ said, as he released his load into her mouth.

Wanna was in the mood to fuck so she swallowed and continued what she was doing. As soon as his dick was hard again, Champ grabbed Wanna and bent her over the sink.

"Damn, these are some pretty panties," he said, as he started to untie the pink and black shear bikinis she was wearing to match her tank.

"Leave them on," Wanna said, as she looked back seductively at Champ, "I want you to fuck me with them on."

Champ pulled the panties to the side and slid his erect dick into Wanna. Initially, he was slow-stroking her but was compelled to fuck her as he watched his reflection in the mirror. The pussy was so good and so wet that he had to hold back his second nut to make sure she got hers. Champ loved the faces that Wanna made when he was fucking her; they forced him to stroke her harder and harder.

"Damn," she said, as she began to throw her pussy back at him.

Champ held her waist and said, "Give it to me, Ma."

The sound of his raspy voice excited her more and she pushed his hands from her waist. Champ looked down to watch as Wanna shook her ass vigorously back and forth on his dick. She bent her body slightly and began clapping her ass cheeks. Champ couldn't take it any longer. He slammed his dick up in her causing Wanna to slap her hand to the mirror.

"Damn, daddy, this dick is so good…uhm…beat this pussy up!" she exclaimed, as she squeezed her pussy tighter on his dick.

"Shit, Wanna, I'm about to cum again."

"Me too, daddy," she barely managed to let out, as her body began to tremble.

The feeling of Wanna's juices dripping from her pussy made Champ bust his nut deep inside of her. He leaned his body over her back and whispered in her ear, "You play too much. I told you I had a meeting."

"Shut up, boy, you enjoyed it," she said, as she gave him a love tap on the chest.

"You got that right. We'll pick up where we left off tonight," Champ said and kissed Wanna on the cheek.

They hopped in the shower to get cleaned up, get dressed, and start their day.

When Champ got in the car, he called Micky and Ducky to let them know he would be an hour late. They knew that Champ was normally punctual so they didn't even attempt to complain. When he pulled up in front of Champions, Ducky and Micky were already inside waiting on him. He went inside, spoke to the staff, and headed back to his usual booth. Micky and Ducky shook his hand and said their 'What's ups'.

Gail was serving them because Champ and Micky both agreed that if Rhonda and Micky were going to be together in a serious relationship then Rhonda shouldn't be waiting tables at Champions. Rhonda put up a fight of course, letting them both know that it wasn't about the paycheck. She definitely came from money. She told them she wanted to work to keep herself both grounded and occupied. She came up with a million excuses for why she should still be able to work, but they all fell on deaf ears. Champ came up with a fair decision after he realized that it hurt her feelings to let the job go. He suggested that she be in charge of the payroll, a job that didn't require her to be at the restaurant dealing with the sometimes thuggish customers. She agreed and everybody was happy, especially Wanna who now had one less job. She had been doing payroll since Champions opened three years ago. The only time Rhonda would have to come to the restaurant would be on Fridays to drop off the paychecks.

Gail took Champ's order and left to get Ducky and Micky's food.

"Champ, you heard about Dawud getting killed?" Ducky asked.

"Yeah, I got a few calls about that Ducky," Champ replied. "It's been a lot of gunplay, and sooner or later the feds are going to step in."

"So, what's our move, big homie?"

"We're going to stay doing us. We're going to get this paper but we're staying away from all the dumb shit. I don't like fucking with them feds; they are some hard motherfuckers to beat. So stay low and keep firing," Champ said, looking from Ducky to Micky then back to Ducky.

"I'm staying in my lane but I'm being honest with you; if I run across the nigga who did Dawud dirty and I got the drop, I'm going to handle the nigga," Ducky said, looking intently at Champ.

Champ respected Ducky and always gave him room to be his own man.

"I hear you, Ducky, and I liked little Dawud, too, but Teddy and them are more than capable of handling this shit. We need to stay in our lane and get our paper."

"Champ, I hear you and I follow you. I didn't say I was looking for the nigga, but if he fell in my lap I'd hit the nigga hard."

"I ain't mad at that. Just don't make it your priority."

"I'm not."

"Anyway, I called y'all to let y'all know that I'm opening up a Champions Two on 52nd and Market and I got room for two solid investors. Y'all are the perfect two to have on my side," Champ offered.

"Man, I don't know nothing about selling no turkey bacon, egg, and cheese sandwiches. I sell bricks, my nigga," Ducky said, laughing but serious as a heart attack.

Champ loved Ducky but this was the one thing that hurt his heart about his main man. Champ was the type that loved his people despite their short comings.

"Ducky, you can't be in the game forever. Eventually, the feds will come and give you forever," Champ said, hoping to get through to his man.

"I hear you, Champ, but I'm not messing with no restaurant. You're good at that type of stuff, not me."

"I respect that, Ducky. What's up with you, Micky?" Champ said, turning to Micky who had been quietly listening.

"I'm with it, Unc. What do I need to get down with it?" Micky asked, not knowing that he had just made Champ proud of him.

"You don't need anything right now. I just need to know that you're down with me and willing to take a step toward building our own shit," Champ said, schooling Micky, and wanting him to want more than what the streets had to offer.

"Unc, you've never steered me wrong, so with me what you say is law," Micky said, with a serious look on his face.

"Champ, fuck it, count me in, too," Ducky said, not wanting to be left out now that Micky jumped in on the offer.

"Damn, Ducky, what made you change your mind so fast?"

"I just don't want this little nigga to blow up without me," Ducky said, grabbing Micky's head and mugging him playfully.

"Ducky, I'm glad you got down, because when it's all said and done I'm trying to have a breakfast store in every hood. I'm trying to shut down all the other ones like Ace's Diner, Let's Grub, Yummy's, and the Breakfast Club."

"Just let me know what you want from me and I'll give it to you," Ducky said, ready to fly now that he made his choice.

"Just like I said, Ducky, y'all don't need anything right now."

They finished their food before Micky paid the bill and tipped Gail with a twenty.

"Thank you, cutie-pie," she said, appreciating the tip.

"Thank you, Ms. Gail," he replied.

The three men went outside so they could get down to their other business. Ducky took the car with the bricks in the stash box and Champ took his car. Micky followed Champ down Delaware Avenue to his warehouse. They pulled up and Champ pressed the security code to raise the gate. They pulled in as the gate came back down.

"Come on, Micky, the car is over here," Champ said, pointing to a black Buick Park Avenue.

"It's $350,000 in the stash box, Unc," Micky said, as he threw Champ the keys to the Honda he got the other day.

"Micky, you're moving good. You're a natural. Don't use no drugs, and you'll go straight to the top of this shit," Champ said, feeling that even at Micky's age he was more capable of running the business than Ducky.

"Unc, I'm just trying to make my mark and be done," Micky said, opening the door of the Park Avenue.

"Just be careful, Micky."

"I will," Micky said, pulling out of the warehouse with a stash box full of bricks.

~~~~~

Teddy and Nino were up all night trying to catch up with Tone. They didn't have concrete information that Tone was behind Dawud's shooting, but he was the only one they had any type of beef with. No matter how many times they tried to come up with another person to blame for Dawud's death, they kept coming up with Tone as their number one suspect.

They had been waiting outside of this little apartment that Tone was known to frequent. After hours of waiting, they decided to roll out.

"Man, I swear I can't wait to hit this nigga," Nino said, holding his gun in his hand.

"Man, we're going to do this nigga for Dawud. I miss his greedy ass," Teddy said, his eyes red from crying all day.

"Yo, did the bitch tell you about any other spots that the nigga be at?"

"Nino, she only gave me this spot right here, but I'll call her and see if she got another spot for us to lay on."

"What about his sister, Nay? Don't that bitch live near Wendy's on Adam's Avenue at them bullshit apartments?" Nino asked, as if it came to him as a revelation.

"Yeah, but do you really think the nigga would hide out there?" Teddy said, skeptically.

"Man, it beats us going in the house without this maggot-ass nigga eating the dirt."

"Okay....let's go over there and see what's up."

"When we catch up to this nigga, we're going to out him and I don't care if the cops are there, I'm laying that maggot out for Dawud," Nino said, wanting a big piece of Tone.

The fact that Dawud had gotten done dirty in broad daylight in front of everybody made it even worse. Everybody was talking, and that put Teddy and Nino in a hell of a position. Everyone knew that Dawud was their boy, so they were waiting on them to make their next move. The ball was in their court and it was up to them to shoot a jumper or lay it up. Whatever they did, they couldn't turn it over.

"Yo, I'm calling Golden Girl's show at midnight to give Dawud a rest in peace shout-out," Nino said, wanting a way to ease his pain.

"Man we're not calling Golden Girl about Dawud. He didn't even listen to Golden Girl. Besides...it's our job to make the maggot-nigga Tone people call and give Tone a rest in peace shout-out."

125

"You're right Teddy. Yo, we got to go get our rest in peace tattoos tomorrow and represent Dawud."

"Yeah, I'm with that. Yo, I was surprised Dawud didn't bust back," Teddy said, as he pulled up to a red light.

"He didn't get a chance to. You know Dawud would have bust his gun with no rap."

"Yeah, Dawud liked playing with them burners more than he liked making money," Teddy said, with a slight smile on his face as he reminisced on his homie.

Teddy turned on Adams Avenue and was surprised by what he saw.

"Damn...you see what I see?" he said, excitedly.

"Yeah, Teddy, make a U-turn," Nino said, when they spotted Tone's Benz turning off Adams Avenue onto the Boulevard. Teddy made a quick u-turn.

"Don't lose that fucking car!" Nino shouted, while putting on his gloves.

"I think that's a bitch driving," Teddy observed.

"It is, but it's a nigga in the passenger side."

"Oh, shit! It *is* a nigga in there. He think he got all the smarts riding in the passenger side," Teddy said, steadying his car behind the Benz.

"We'll see how smart he is when his brains are on the dash board. Pull up beside that motherfucker right now," Nino yelled.

Teddy pulled beside the Benz, and before the occupants knew what happened, Nino had his A-R-15 out the window.

Mock...mock...mock!

The fully-loaded automatic weapon went at rapid speed riddling the Benz and it's passengers with bullets. The Benz hit a tree and came to a stop. Cars were beeping their horns and people were ducking out of the way. It was pure chaos.

Teddy stepped on the gas peddle of the Charger and the hemi engine roared. He made it his business to get off the Boulevard and take the streets of North Philly back down to West. The Boulevard was always full of highway patrol, so Teddy knew that his best chance of getting away with the shooting was to stay off the Boulevard.

"Damn, nigga, you hit them the fuck up, my nigga."

"What the fuck...I told you I was going to do it for Dawud. Fuck Tone, I hope he dies two times over," Nino said, now relieved because he had the opportunity to bust his gun for Dawud.

"I'm with you, Nino. That nigga, Tone, is taking a dirt nap and eating mud patties." They both laughed at Teddy's comment.

They made their way to the clubhouse on Markoe Street and calmly walked in, leaving the burners in the car. Teddy went right to the refrigerator and pulled out two Coronas. He popped the top on his and passed the other to Nino. After a few guzzles of the beer, they were both settled.

"Yo, I wonder if Dawud could see me busting my shit for him from the sky. *Mock, mock, mock*," Nino blurted out, while pointing his fingers in the shape of a gun.

"I don't know if he saw you...but I did, and I know that he's resting in peace," Teddy said, guzzling the rest of his beer.

"Yeah, you know how that goes...kill my dog and I'll slay your cat," replied Nino.

"I'm going home to see if Lisa will give me some pussy tonight. What are you going to do?"

"I'm going home, too. I'm not staying here."

"Cool, I'll get up with you in the a.m.," Teddy said.

They both got into their cars leaving the Charger parked on Markoe Street.

~~~~~

Micky had been spending a lot of time with Rhonda. He hustled all day with Toot, but his nights were shared with Rhonda. Toot was his homie, but Rhonda was becoming his new best friend. The sex they shared was great, but their relationship wasn't just about sex. They'd learned to trust each other with their secrets, and told each other just about everything. They shared long and short-term goals. Rhonda wasn't judgmental about Micky's lifestyle, and she appreciated that he had ghosts. She never met a nigga his age with his drive and swagger.

On top of all that, Rhonda even enjoyed hanging out with his family. She was spending a lot of time with Micky's mom, Sharon, and his aunt, Wanna. Rhonda considered Micky's family to be a host of genuine people. Of course, like everybody else, she couldn't stand Tone.

One day, when she was over Sharon's for dinner with Micky, she was sitting in the living room patting Cavalli while Micky was in the kitchen talking to Sharon. Tone pretended to be taking Cavalli off her lap and rubbed his hand across her pelvis. She wanted to tell Micky so badly, but didn't want to be the cause of any pain for Sharon. She avoided going over Sharon's ever since because Tone creeped her out.

Micky had been staying with her at her apartment right off campus. He didn't move in with her. He kept his apartment, which Toot basically took over because he was there more than Micky. Micky thought it was too early to move in with Rhonda despite the fact that he was there a lot, so he forced himself to stay home at times.

"Dinner was good, Micky," said Rhonda.

"Yeah, I love that teriyaki chicken at Hibachis," Micky said, sitting on the edge of the bed.

"That was good, but then again, everything is good with you, Micky."

"What do you mean by that?" he asked.

Rhonda sat down on the bed next to him.

"I mean, we could have had hot dogs...as long as I had them with you they would have been good. When we hang up the phone or when you leave out and I say that I love you, I mean it. Icky, huh? I don't know how all of this happened. It all happened fast, too fast for real, but I wouldn't change it for nothing in the world. I love you, Micky," Rhonda said, a little tipsy and a whole lot emotional.

"Rhonda, real rap...this shit happened overnight for me, too. Shit is going so smooth with us and with my life that it scares the fuck out of me. You want to hear something crazy? I've always fought my feelings when it came to women, and I've never given my heart to a girl, but it seems like you are literally taking it out of my chest. What's crazier is that I don't have the desire to fight it," Micky said, as he kicked off his Louis Vuitton sneakers.

"Micky, all I had was my parents. I didn't have a big family, but it seems like you have given me one. Your mom and Wanna are the best. Your Uncle Champ is a good man. The only one who brings about negative energy is Tone," she said, watching his reaction.

"Yeah, my mom and aunt love you. I don't know what you did to them but they are really feeling you. As far as

Tone, he's okay. He's just stuck in his ways," Micky said, stripping down to his drawers.

Rhonda leaned over and lightly kissed his lips, deciding to keep Tone's transgression to herself for the moment. Micky kissed her back and inserted his tongue in her mouth. They kissed passionately while rubbing all over each other's body.

Micky laid her on her back and stripped her naked. Rhonda had the perfect body. Her perfect titties sat up without a trace of sagging. Her hips were small and her heart-shaped ass looked like it was molded out of clay. Micky sucked on her titties working his way down to her waistline. She was moaning and squirming. She was so turned on she wondered what Micky's tongue would feel like up in her. She knew how good his dick felt in her, but she never felt his tongue. Her curiosity was put to rest when she felt Micky's tongue on her clit.

She had heard stories of how good it felt to be pleased this way, but she never knew the real thing. She felt like she was in heaven. Micky licked the inside of her pussy and then sucked on the clit hard while popping her pussy with his middle finger. She couldn't take it anymore. Her legs were shaking as she had the biggest orgasm in her life.

Micky slid on his magnum condom and began fucking her from the back. He could feel the wetness of her pussy despite the condom. He turned her over onto her back, put her legs on his shoulders, inserted his dick inside her, and began pounding her pussy with long, deep, hard strokes.

She began shaking again, saying, "Damn, Micky...I love you. This dick is so good."

"This pussy is the best. I'm about to cum," Micky said, while his body began to shake from his orgasm. After he

came he took the condom off, and they went to sleep with
Rhonda's head nestled on Micky's chest.

Chapter 13

Tone had murder on his mind. He blamed everybody for his sister getting shot. He planned on getting at everyone he believed was against him.

It was early in the morning when Bernadette called him with news of Nay getting shot. He saw that a lady got shot and her passenger was killed on the news, but he never imagined that the victim was his sister. Despite the fact that Nay was ignorant, and that she took his car against his will, she was still his only sibling and he loved her to death. Tone was going to get Sab so he could start putting their moves down.

He pulled into the hospital parking lot thinking of how his sister ended up in the same hospital in which he spent weeks after he got shot. When he walked into the lobby, he saw Sharon and a few other people he knew.

"Where's my mom?" Tone asked Sharon, who walked up to him as soon as she saw him.

"She's back there with Nay," Sharon said.

Tone neglected to say anything else to Sharon. He walked away and left her standing there. He got the room number from the nurse and walked toward the back.

When he entered the room he saw Bernadette leaning over Nay's bed talking to Nay who appeared to be asleep. Nay was heavily sedated because of the pain from the bullet wounds.

"Mom, what's up with Nay?" Tone said, startling his mom who didn't even notice he walked into the room.

"Boy...I didn't even see you there. She's okay. She got two flesh wounds. The doctor said the bullets went in and out, but they want to keep her to run some tests."

"Damn, this shit is crazy. Somebody is going to pay for shooting my baby sis," Tone said, looking at his sister who lay in the hospital bed, all banged up.

Bernadette turned her son shaking her head.

"Anthony, watch your mouth. Leave this in the hands of the lord. You and this girl are going to give me a heart attack."

"Mom, my fault for cursing, but I can't believe somebody would shoot Nay," Tone said, trying to make sense of what happened to his sister.

"The police came by here talking about they have some questions for you because you were known to drive the car she was shot in. You know her boyfriend died, Anthony?"

"The police? What else did they say?"

"They said that you know them and the little nice one gave me this card for you," Bernadette said, passing Tone the card with Detective Hutson's name on it.

"The nice one? Mom, it ain't nothing nice about this cop. He's a prick."

"Well he was nice to me, he even sent the other one to get me this here soda," Bernadette said, holding up her soda.

"Mom, I'll call you later to check on y'all. I have a lot to do. Tell Nay I said I love her," Tone said.

He kissed his mom on the cheek and rolled out. When he got to the lobby, Sharon ran over to him.

"How are you? Was Nay awake when you went in there?" Sharon said, trying to provide Tone some comfort.

"Bitch, don't ask me about my sister. You don't even like her. If I hadn't chosen you over her she would of never took that car and she wouldn't have gotten shot," Tone said, blaming Nay's injuries on Sharon.

Sharon was embarrassed, too embarrassed to say or do anything. She broke into tears as she noticed that all eyes were on her. She rushed out the hospital fed up with Tone and all his shit. She promised herself that this would be the last time Tone would humiliate her.

Tone strolled out of the hospital. He needed his medicine. His desire to get snorted was bad. When he got to the parking lot, he got pissed when he saw someone leaning up against his car. When he got closer, he realized that it was Starsky and Hutch.

"What the fuck do y'all want and why are y'all leaning on my shit?" he snarled.

"Well...we saw you going into the hospital, but because we are your friends, we didn't want to disturb you while you were visiting your sister. Since this is important, we decided to wait on you out here," Starks said, with his wicked smile.

"I don't feel like this shit today. I'm not y'alls friend today and I wont be y'alls friend tomorrow," Tone retorted.

"Oh, you should take any friend you can get because a birdie told us that the person who shot Nay and killed her boyfriend was really trying to get you," Detective Hutson said, speaking over Tone and Starks.

"The way I feel right now, I wish they'd hurry the fuck up. I got y'alls card...how about I give y'all a call later,"

Tone said, while holding up the card he got from his mom for the cops to see.

"Tone, you can play games and not get with us if you want. Your name has been coming up in a whole lot of shit and it will only be but so long before we can get something to stick," Starks said, truthfully.

Many of the local informants put Tone's name in a lot of shit that's been happening, but they just couldn't prove it. It didn't matter because assumptions were all the police needed to jump on your ass.

"I'll call y'all," Tone said, as he hit his remote to open his car doors.

"You better," Hutson said, getting up off the car allowing Tone to get in. Tone pulled off with no intention of getting back to them dickheads.

Tone headed over the bridge to pick up his main man, Sab. He called Sab's phone when he turned onto his block off Mount Ephraim Avenue. Sab came out and jumped in the car eating a cup of noodles.

"What's up, my nigga?" Sab said, slurping the hot noodles.

"It ain't shit, my nigga. God damn...slow down on the noodles before you choke," Tone advised.

"Man, it's fucked up out here and all a nigga got to keep him alive is a mother-fucking cup of noodles," Sab said, letting Tone know that he basically needed a check.

Sab and Tone barely hustled as of late, and Sab needed the thousand dollar profit he was making off of each brick he used to sell to his Camden niggas for Tone.

"I know niggas got to eat. I got you, baby bro," Tone assured him, "I'm going to hit you with some paper tonight after we put this work in."

"That's what a nigga is talking about. I need that chicken to go with these noodles," Sab said, referring to the money Tone had promised him.

"Yo, somebody shot Nay last night and killed her boyfriend while she was driving my car up the Boulevard," Tone told Sab, who paused before he responded.

"Yeah, that's fucked up," he said, "Do you think it was behind the nigga we put the dirt on at the Chinese store?"

"I don't know, but we're going to put the press on every motherfucker in Philly who even acts funny toward me," Tone said, stopping at the red light with a bag of coke in his hand and a dollar rolled up as a quill to snort it.

"Man, I'm with you, and we can do it on the late night or broad daylight. I don't give a fuck," Sab said, reaching for the bag of coke.

Now Sab could get high all day for free. Sab was still a little bitter about the way Tone pressed him and Dave to get at Boop, which in turn cost Dave his life, but Tone and Sab had grown a little closer from being together everyday and snorting their problems away.

"Sab, we got to get at these niggas, and once we're done, we're going to bring all the work over to Camden and flood your hood with all raw."

"Well, let's hurry up and get all of this shit out of the way then," Sab said, falling for yet another dream Tone was selling him.

Sab knew Tone was selfish and that he always sold dreams, but Sab hoped that one day Tone would come through and really let him eat.

"Them pussies shot Nay. That's Tone's sister...I'm fucking Tough-Tony. Them cockroaches must have lost their fucking minds," Tone said, going through his Scarface act as a result of the coke kicking in.

"Yeah, they crossed the line. They shot Nay like she was some nigga in the street," Sab said, thinking of Nay and her good pussy. Sab snuck behind Tone's back plenty of times to fuck Nay.

"I got something for all of them. Do they think they can get out on Tone and not get dealt with?" Tone said, high as fuck and referring to himself in the third person.

They drove by the tire shop but it was closed.

"How the fuck is the tire shop closed on a weekday? Every motherfucker needs tires. I know these coward-ass niggas ain't hiding from me. Y'all motherfuckers shot my sister and now y'all hiding," Tone yelled, actually talking to the closed tire shop as he pulled off.

Sab was wired off the raw coke thinking, *This nigga Tone is losing his fucking mind.*

"Yo, we're riding over to that whack-ass pool hall, and if we see Bingo or Teddy we are going to kill them pussies on the spot."

"Whatever you want to do we're going to do," Sab said, playing yes-man just to get his hands on Tone's coke. They got to the pool hall and the cops were coming out with computers, safes, and all types of documents.

"Damn...what the fuck is going on in that joint? The feds are all over that motherfucker," Tone said, driving by scared as shit because they had guns in the car. When he saw Starsky and Hutch dick-eating the feds in the middle of the street he really started bitching and praying that they didn't see him.

~~~~~

138

Champ and Wanna were out getting something to eat when he received a phone call from Thelma. She sounded scared and talked quickly in a near panic. Champ had to tell her three times to calm down, and once she told him what she wanted, he agreed to meet her.

Champ would never let a loved one down, especially not Thelma. Thelma was undoubtedly his best cousin. She was his biggest advocate and everybody knew it.

One time, Tone tried to play her in the hairdresser. He called her little Champ and Thelma sounded him so badly he had to calm her down by saying that he was just playing. She knew he wasn't playing, but since he basically bitched up, she used the attention to let everybody in the shop know where she stood.

She said, "If Champ say a mosquito can fly a plane, I'm going to put the mosquito in the cockpit. It's Champ's world and I think y'all should be happy that I let y'all live in it."

Although Tone and a few other niggas hated her for that statement, they knew better than to get into it, because she's the type that will keep going until you end up smacking her. That would mean all out war, so they let her have the floor and kept their comments to themselves.

When Champ got word of what happened, he told Thelma to keep her cool....what's understood in the streets doesn't need to be spoken on. Everybody knew Thelma was riding with Champ until the end, and when Ern got killed, it was understood that Champ would eventually pass Tone and Bingo. He didn't discuss his paper, instead he let it speak for itself, and that's what he had to get across to Thelma back then. She eventually understood what he was trying to tell her. Today's conversation was about her husband not her cousin. She had the same hurt in her speech as if it was Champ that got locked up.

When Champ pulled up her driveway, she really got the sense of comfort she needed.

"You can come in, boo," Champ said, putting the car in park and looking at Wanna.

They got out and walked up to the door Thelma held open when she spotted them getting out of the car. When they entered the ransacked house, Champ automatically felt bad for his cousin. Thelma ran over to Champ. He hugged her as she broke into tears. She didn't say anything, she just held on to her cousin, the center of her life, like he was her security blanket.

Wanna felt so bad for Thelma, but at that moment, she realized just how much Champ meant to everyone.

"What's up, Cousin? Tell me what happened and what you need," Champ said, sitting Thelma down and wrapping an arm around her.

"Cousin, the FBI, ATF, and the DEA came in here early this morning with all these guns waving at me and Bingo. They had a warrant and searched the whole house. They took Bingo. They said he is being indicted along with three other men on a four-count indictment," Thelma told them, "Cousin, they seized the pool hall, the tire shop, our accounts, and all our properties except this one. The lady cop said it was because this was solely in my name. There was no complaint of criminal activity involving this address, so they didn't involve this in the seizure," Thelma continued, getting herself together by wiping her eyes and blowing her nose with the tissue Wanna got her from the bathroom.

"Damn, baby-girl, them fucking feds can make life hard for Bingo. Did you call the lawyer yet?" asked Champ.

"Yeah, I called Fred Perri, and you know he didn't want to talk on the phone, so I have to go down there this evening. You know he's going to want an arm and a leg and these people froze everything," she replied.

"Cousin, this is me. I would do it for Bingo with no rap if he wasn't with my favorite cousin. We have a lot of problems, but money is not one of them," Champ said, hugging his cousin as if she was his daughter.

Champ was relieved that Bingo respected his wishes and didn't involve his cousin in the streets.

"Cousin, as soon as I talk to him face to face I'll find out where the cash is so I can give you the lawyer money back," Thelma promised.

"Thelma, I'm not worrying about no lawyer money. As long as you're good and he gets a fair chance at beating them people, I'm cool," Champ told her.

"Do you want me to go to the lawyer's office with her?" Wanna offered, being supportive to Thelma and letting Champ know that she was at his service.

"Yeah, go with her and then y'all can meet back up with me later on," Champ said, taking her up on her offer.

"Cousin, I don't want to stay here by myself tonight," Thelma said, looking around the house, which looked like it was hit by a tornado.

"Thelma, you can stay at our crib until you're ready to come back here. Just forward your house phone to your cell so you can catch his call," Champ said, kissing Thelma on the cheek.

He hugged his favorite two women and they exited the house. Thelma and Wanna jumped in Thelma's Porsche

Cayenne and headed downtown to visit one of the best lawyers in the city, both lost in their own thoughts of how much Champ meant to them.

Champ was in his GTC on his way to meet Micky and Toot. His thoughts were in overdrive on how he was going to shake the streets. Although he ran a smooth operation, he knew the feds would exhaust all their resources to get at any nigga they wanted. He knew his legit success was very lucrative and the paper trail was solid, but he also knew anything could happen at any given time in the streets. He never did any business with Bingo although he had lent Bingo money in the past. This was a wake up call because it was so close to home. Champ had to speed up his exit plan to get out of the game.

When he pulled up to Micky's apartment, he called Micky and told him to open the door. Champ parked the whip and went inside, not noticing hating-ass Tone pulling away from the curb in front of the apartment.

When he got inside, he noticed Micky looked upset.

"What's up, nephew? What's the mean face for?" Champ asked.

"Ain't shit, Unc. This nigga, Tone, is a stupid motherfucker and I'm not feeling him."

"Yeah, what did he do now?" Champ asked, concerned about Micky.

"He came by here unannounced and brought his lame-ass man with him. I been told him not to bring nobody past the spot because I don't trust the niggas he fucks with. I thought it was you, so I told Toot to go open the door, and Tone came in here on some newsy shit looking around. I had a little ten thousand lying on the table so he's like, 'Damn y'all niggas are getting money without me'."

I told him we're not doing shit. Eventually, he left but he turned me off bringing his man, Sab, in here," Micky said, his face balled-up the whole time.

"Yeah, don't keep no paper in here from now on, and, as soon as you can, move out of this jawn."

"Tone looks bad. He lost like 30 pounds and his beard was nappy. He looked like he had the same clothes on for days and he was stinking," Toot said.

"Naw...not Tone. I need to catch up with him to see what's up with the nigga. He can't look that bad," Champ said in disbelief.

"Champ, that's my family so you know I wouldn't lie on him. The nigga looks fucked up," Toot insisted, saddened by his own words.

"Damn, that's crazy. If y'all want, I got a loft on Delaware Avenue where I used to go just to fuck chicks. I don't use it now 'cause I'm good with my chick I got now, so y'all can have it if y'all want."

"Unc, that's what's up! We'll try to get up in there as soon as possible," Micky said, with appreciation.

"No problem...I'll tell Ducky to give y'all the keys."

"We were out with Ducky and crazy-ass Raheem the other day," Toot said, excited about the fun they had at Scooters the other night.

"Yo, I wanted to tell y'all that Bingo got booked by the feds. The streets might open up a little more with his people that didn't get booked looking for work. Y'all are doing enough. Y'all don't need no new traffic...all money is not good money," Champ said, talking to Toot as well as Micky.

At first Champ was hesitant to deal with Toot, but since Micky insisted that Toot's loyalty was to them, Champ gave Toot the benefit of the doubt.

"What did they book him for, and did they book Teddy and Nino with him?" Micky asked.

"I don't know exactly what happened. I'll know a little more tonight and I'll let y'all know what's up tomorrow," Champ assured him.

"Damn, we were all just out partying at Onyx and now they're booked," Toot said, thinking of how the night at Onyx was the best night of his life.

"Yeah, little homie, that's how this street shit go so you got to stay three steps ahead of the law, four steps ahead of the kidnappers, and a mile ahead of the killers, and even with all that distance, still know that you're never far enough ahead of any of them," Champ said, dropping a verbal jewel on the youngsters.

He gave them both a handshake and was out. He got in his car and went to holler at Ducky.

~~~~~

Tone and Sab were running the streets all day. Tone called Sharon acting like he was being nice so he could execute his new plan since he found out Bingo and them got indicted. He promised himself that, when he finished with his plan, he would kill Sharon, too. He reasoned with himself that the pussy was too good and he had invested too much into her to let her be with another nigga. Tone told her he would be home tonight and that he wanted to do whatever it took to make sure their relationship worked. Sharon, being the sucker for Tone that she was, fell for his lies and allowed herself to believe Tone was ready to get it together.

Tone pulled up to the tire shop and let Sab out. Sab scurried over to the building and busted the window out. He lit a pre-made gas cocktail and threw it inside the window before he ran back to the car. By the time they reached the corner, they could see the tire shop up in flames.

"Faggot-ass nigga trying to hid in jail after they shot my sister. Faggots take that!" Tone shouted, with a wicked laugh.

"Fuck'em, baby-boy... fuck'em," Sab said, enjoying all the drama.

They pulled up to the side of the Chinese store where heaps of teddy bears and candles marked Dawud's memorial. Sab got out with his burner in hand for insurance in the event someone tried to stop him. He poured lighter fluid on the teddy bears and set them aflame. He ran and jumped back into the car. By the time the people on the next corner realized what happened, Dawud's memorial was up in flames.

Tone pulled off laughing.

"Fuck'em, baby...fuck'em" Sab said, while snorting some coke.

"Sab, we are going to fuck this city up if it's the last thing we do," Tone declared.

"I'm with you. It's me and you against the world," Sab said.

"Fuck'em baby...fuck'em," Tone said, mimicking Sab's earlier statement. The two laughed all the way to the pool hall where Sab threw another lit gas cocktail through the window. The pool hall went up in flames.

Tone took Sab back home to Jersey. They snorted coke the entire ride as they took turns saying 'fuck'em baby, fuck'em'.

Tone gave Sab $5,000 and promised to come get him tomorrow. It was a long day and Tone was tired. He went home to Sharon, but he no longer wanted her for her but for any information she possessed.

Chapter 14

Bingo had never experienced anything like the federal detention center in his life. The food was garbage and the staff was ignorant for the most part. There were a few guards and counselors that were cool but the majority of them were nasty. Everyone was lumped into one pot. They didn't know a dope fiend from a dope pusher or a peon from a don. You were simply a nigga in a jumpsuit to them. You couldn't really trust too many niggas because everyone was facing massive time, so niggas would jump on other peoples' cases to get their personal time cut.

You could only use the phone once every hour and you could only use three hundred minutes a month. Your visitor list could only consist of immediate family and one friend. There was no diversity since you were stuck on the same block all day. As a result, you had to socialize solely with the niggas on your block. There was a way you could talk to people on other floors but you had to make sure you didn't get caught by the guards. In order to do so, you had to clear all the water out of your toilet as well as the cell it was connected to on the floor above or below. Then you could talk loud and clear.

A lot of dudes had bowl girlfriends. The females were housed on the third floor so they would holler up on the bowl and get them a boyfriend to talk to throughout the day. Some people did it to help their time pass but others really thought they were in a relationship.

Bingo, Teddy, and Nino were blessed to be on the same block. Normally co-defendants were split up so they could be divided and conquered by the system. Even if your co-defendant was not snitching, the separation and inability to discuss things with one another made you start thinking crazy. Bingo had this crazy thought about one of their co-defendants, Joe-baby, a Spanish cat that he had been serving for years. They were all brought to the jail together but, when it came to being assigned to a block, Joe was the only one that was separated. The C.O. said that it was due to a government separation. All this shit was brand new to Bingo. He just wanted to see his lawyer and Thelma and get a peace of mind.

"Yo, I talked to my wife and she said that the lawyer will be up here today and we have court tomorrow," Bingo said.

"Damn, we got to see what this shit is all about. I can't believe they just came and scooped us like that and didn't say shit," Teddy said, looking out of Bingo's window.

"Once we get to see our lawyers, we'll get some idea of what's going on. I told Thelma to Western Union both of y'all $500 a piece for y'alls accounts," Bingo told Teddy and Nino.

"I don't know what to think about Jay-baby," Bingo said, confused about the separation.

"Damn, I hope Thelma hurries up with the money so I can use the phone and we can fill out these commissary slips for tomorrow," Nino finally said.

"That's good as gold. Thelma is going to get right on top of that," Bingo said, knowing his wife would do the right thing.

"Do you think Jay-baby will tell on us?" Teddy said, concerned about the separation.

"Naw...I don't think he would tell," Bingo replied, "Besides, he only did business with me so y'all're straight as far as he goes. Did y'all have anything at y'alls cribs they ran in?"

"Naw, just money?" Teddy said, speaking for himself and Nino, knowing that the last of the coke they had was sold the day Dawud died.

"That's good. I only had money, too, so we're just fighting the investigation at this point," Bingo said, relieved that there shouldn't have been any coke found by the police.

Just as he finished talking there was a knock on the cell door. All three men looked at the stranger on the other side of the door.

"May I enter?" the man asked, in accordance to custom when a Muslim desires to enter the living space of another man.

"Come in," Bingo said, waving his hand.

"Which one of y'all is Bingo from down the bottom?" the man asked.

"I'm Bingo," Bingo answered, not feeling threatened by the man's approach but pretty strong about him and his team winning three against one if it came down to it.

"I'm Shaahir from Up-Town. Champ is like family to me and he told me to check on you."

"Yeah, Champ is my man. Thanks for checking on me," Bingo said.

"I know y'all won't need anything once y'all get settled in but this is for y'all and if y'all need anything else let me know. I'm in 13-cell," Shaahir said, knowing that if they were Champ's people they would not need anything once they got settled. Plus, he had heard of Bingo through the streets so he knew he had his own.

"Thanks, main man, but we can't take that," Bingo said, returning laundry bag full of food, toiletries, shower shoes, and walkmans.

"Would you take it if Champ brought it in here to you?" Shaahir asked.

Bingo shook his head, "Yeah, because that's my folks."

"He's my folks, too, and I owe him countless favors," Shaahir told him, "He asked me to look out for y'all so I can't take it back. Don't ask these suckers for nothing. If y'all need something, be sure to come to me. Peace," he said, dropping the bag of necessities on the floor.

Shaahir was Champ's man since way back. As soon as Shaahir left the cell, Teddy started going through the bag.

"What did you mean we wouldn't take this? You're crazy," Teddy said, breaking the items down into threes.

"I don't know, dude, and I'm not with a hand-out. The way he broke down the scenario about *if it were Champ giving me the bag* made me look at the situation differently."

"I wouldn't have cared if he said Eddie Murphy told him to bring us the bag...I was accepting it," Nino said, dead serious.

Bingo and Teddy busted out laughing. After they showered, they all went to the dayroom and watched the 12 o'clock news. Before they could get into a full conversation about the report on the burnings at the tire shop and pool hall, Bingo was called on a legal visit.

~~~~~

Tone got a little information from Sharon. He got the fact that Bingo got indicted from her. She told him that Wanna didn't tell her who else was indicted. He figured he would stay alert as if Teddy and Nino were still on the streets until he got confirmation that they were booked, too.

He also learned from her that Micky'd been with Champ a lot and he asked her to get him a new car. He got jealous when she told him that Micky wanted her to sign for a Maserati. Tone almost had a heart attack when she informed him that Micky would be trading in his Lexus to get the car and that Champ would be paying off the balance owed.

Tone went and picked up his main man, Sab, with a whole new wicked mission. They went to see Nay in the hospital. She was awake and alert when Tone entered the room.

"What's up, Nay? How are you, baby-girl?" Tone asked with concern evident in his voice.

"I'm good Tone, I guess. I'm not dead, so I guess I can't complain."

"Do you need anything, Sis?"

"No, I just need to get out of here."

"Be easy, you'll be out of here soon," he assured her.

"Not soon enough," she replied, "Tone, them clown-ass detectives were here early this morning asking a lot of questions about you."

"What did you tell them?" Tone asked, a little concerned about what Nay would have to say, especially since their last conversation wasn't so pleasant.

"I didn't tell them shit," Nay said, to Tone's relief.

"That's good...I hate the fucking cops," he said.

"Me, too," said Nay, in agreement.

"I'm out, Nay. I'll see you when you get home," Tone said, kissing his sister on the cheek before he rolled out.

When Tone got into the car, he decided it was time to put today's plan into motion.

"Sab, do you know those fucking niggas, Toot and Micky, crossed us?"

"No…why do you say that?" Sab said, not wanting to believe it.

"Them niggas are getting money with Champ."

"Your homie, Champ?" Sab said, a little confused.

"Yeah, that nigga, Champ, got the niggas eating. Micky is trying to get a Maserati in Sharon's name. That little nigga don't even have a job," Tone said, snorting from a bag of coke they had.

"We can't hurt the young-bucks, Tone," said Sab.

"We won't hurt them little niggas, but we are going up in that crib and take that paper they got."

"What if they don't want to give it up?"

"We're going to go when they're not there, but if it comes down to it and they're there, fuck it. We'll just have to do them like you did Micky's dad," Tone said, now high and bringing up the fact that he paid Sab five years ago to get rid of Ern so he could get the connect and possibly Sharon in the process. The fact that Sab lived over in Jersey made their secret easy to keep between them.

"Yo, sometimes I think Micky can see through the mask I had on that day because he gives me crazy looks," Sab said, now snorting the powder.

"That little nigga ain't see shit. Plus, what the fuck can he do to two gangsters?" Tone said, patting his chest.

"Yeah, fuck it now…we can't bring the little nigga's dad back."

They drove to Micky's apartment snorting and talking shit. They waited outside for over an hour before Sab got out of the car to go in. Tone waited in the car to make sure Micky didn't pull up. After waiting on Sab for about thirty minutes, Tone decided to go in. When he got inside, he couldn't believe what he saw.

"What the fuck are you doing, Sab?" Tone said to Sab, who appeared to be fucking a battered and unconscious Rhonda.

"This bitch was in here packing clothes. I pulled out the burner and told her not to move. The bitch tried to play hero, so I cracked her in the head a few times with the burner, and since the bitch is bad, I sampled the pussy while she was unconscious," Sab said, now standing up and buckling his jeans.

"We got to get the fuck out of here," Tone said, pulling Sab's arm toward the door.

"Let's find the money," Sab said, pulling away and heading toward the closet.

"Fuck the money...we're out!" Tone shouted, as he ran out the door.

Sab followed him. They drove in silence for a while with the music off, taking snorts.

"Nigga, you fucked up for us," Tone said, feeling his high.

"Tone, I don't know why you're bitchin'. She didn't see you. I cracked the bitch in the head so hard with the burner that she might not remember me," Sab said, high out of his mind.

"Damn, we got to step this shit up now because, if them little niggas find out you raped the bitch, they are going to call the cops on us, my nigga."

"We're good, Tone, just relax. The bitch don't know me and I'm the last person that Micky'd think would come in his crib."

They were quiet for a minute.

"Damn, how was the pussy?" Tone asked him, "I wanted that little bitch myself, but I wasn't going to take the pussy. You're a wild little nigga."

"Tone, the pussy wasn't even wet yet. I had just put my dick in her when you came and stopped the show."

"Shiiiit, you were pumping fast as shit when I walked in."

They both shared a laugh.

"You know, after all this shit we got to kill that bitch, Sharon. I'll call to see what's being said once this little bitch go to the hospital and Micky calls his mom. You know he's like Jody off of Baby Boy, always crying to his mom," Tone said, seriously.

~~~~~

Champ was waiting on Wanna to pick him up from Ducky's detail shop. He knew traffic was a little crazy and that she would be a little late, but he wasn't sweating it because he used the extra time to kick it with Ducky and Raheem.

"Ducky, what's the deal with Raheem?" he asked.

"He's good, why?" Ducky asked.

"Because every time I come through he's asleep."

"That nigga be out all night, every night," Ducky informed him.

"Yo, you know Bingo got indicted?" Champ asked, changing the subject.

"Yeah, and some other cat is on their case as well," Ducky replied.

"That's crazy, because them feds be on some other shit," said Champ.

"I'm glad you know that."

"Ducky, our shit is airtight, keep it that way, and stay on point. You're my point guard, you're controlling the rock."

"Champ, I'm here to stay and I'm on top of this shit."

"Did you see the news today?" Champ said, looking out of the window.

"Naw, I've been running around taking care of my business. Why, what happened?" Ducky asked.

"They said somebody set Bingo's pool hall and tire shop on fire."

"Damn...that's some faggot shit."

"Niggas are trying to kick a nigga when he's down," Champ said, not feeling how niggas were trying to get out on Bingo while he was booked.

"Man, I'm keeping it real. I think faggot-ass Tone is behind this shit. Ever since his punk-ass got shot and Bam's bitch's ass got rocked, the nigga Tone has been on some hide-out shit. Every time I turn around, he's in the middle of some he say/she say shit. I don't like the nigga, and if you didn't always tell me to chill, I would have rocked his bitch ass," Ducky said, revealing his true feelings.

"Rock who? Let's get 'em," Raheem said, jumping up out of his sleep not know what they were talking about.

He just heard Ducky talking about rocking somebody and he was on it.

"I'm glad you could join us," Champ said.

"Damn, Champ, when did you get here?"

"I've been here, sleepyhead," Champ told him.

"So, who are we rocking, y'all?"

155

"Nobody," Champ answered, looking at Ducky.

"Oh…well I'm going back to sleep then, niggas. Wake me up when you want me to rock something, my niggas," Raheem said, pulling the sheet over his head.

"That nigga is crazy," Champ said.

He had love for Raheem and, even though he wasn't as good a hustler as Ducky, he was still Champ's boy. Champ and Ducky got back to their conversation.

"Yo, it's crazy because I was just saying that all the feds ran down on Teddy and them," Champ told him.

"Yeah, you called that shit," said Ducky.

"If we don't have to fuck with them guns, we're not going to be shooting them for no reason," Champ said, "Now, if a nigga got to get it, then we're going to bust some asses," he concluded.

"Champ, you don't play with them guns because you're scared," Ducky said, laughing.

"Ducky, I put work in…I just know that the shit don't go with getting money. Look at Gotti, JBM, BMF, Skinny Joey Marleno, Nikki Scarfo, Supreme, and all the different crews that were getting money for years. The feds didn't shut down none of their shit until gunplay became involved. Sure, they'll book you for the drugs and shit, but if it's a lot of gunplay they come down faster and harder."

"Damn, I never even looked at it like that," said Ducky.

"Yo, Wanna just pulled up. I'm out. I'll see you later on," Champ said, before he left.

Champ jumped into the car and gave Wanna a peck on the lips.

"Damn, that's all I get?" Wanna said, poking her lips out. Champ leaned over and French-kissed her. Now satisfied, she pulled off.

"Did you go get the certified check for Thelma to take to the lawyer?" he asked her.

"Yes, Sweetie, and she already took it to him."

"That's what's up. I hope Bingo made out okay."

"I do, too, Champ. Thelma really appreciates how you came through for her boy. You are one-of-a-kind, Sweetie," Wanna said, expressing admiration for her boy.

"Wanna, I know Thelma loves dude, and plus if it were vice versa I know Bingo would have come through for us."

"That's why whatever it is that you're doing you should stop so we don't have to go through what they're going through. I couldn't imagine life without you, Champ," Wanna said.

"Boo, I'm almost done," he assured her, "Believe me, if the feds were to come for me today or tomorrow, they wouldn't be able to touch none of the legit shit we got because I don't mix my dirty paper with my clean paper and I don't do business at my legit spots. I never bring the shit around you, so if shit was to hit the fan you would be more than able to come rescue me."

"And you better know I'll be right there," Wanna assured him back, as she turned onto the Valley Forge exit headed to the King of Prussia Mall. She could drive there with her eyes closed she was there that often.

"Answer my phone...it's Sharon. Tell her I'll call her when I get off the expressway," Wanna said, knowing it was Sharon from the ring tone.

"Hello…slow down, Sharon, you're talking too fast. Where's Micky at? What hospital? We'll meet y'all up there, okay? Bye-bye, baby-girl," he said, all at once.

"What's wrong with Sharon?" Wanna said, because she could only hear Champ's side of the conversation.

"She said that she's on her way to Albert Einstein Medical Center at Broad and Olney."

"Is she okay? What happened?" Wanna asked, beginning to worry.

"She said that somebody hurt Rhonda and Micky is on his way to take her to the hospital."

"What happened to my Rhonda? She's a sweetheart. Who would hurt her?" Wanna asked, pulling off the Conshohocken exit and turning the car around to go back to Philly.

"I don't know what's going on but I'm sure Micky is mad as all outdoors," Champ said, as his phone rang. It was Micky.

"What's up, nephew? I just talked to your mom. I'm on my way with Wanna to meet y'all at the hospital," Champ said, not giving Micky a chance to talk recklessly on the phone.

Champ hung up. He wasn't being rude, he just knew that when a man's woman or family is involved, emotions tend to run high. Although he knew he did an excellent job of schooling Micky, he knew that Micky was still young and young bulls running high off emotions get a little reckless unless they're stopped in their tracks by someone who could show them better.

"Baby, it's been a good time for us getting to know each other as a couple but it's been so ugly for the people around us," said Wanna.

"Wanna, you're right, but what can we do but ride it out? Life is full of ups and downs. We got to roll with the punches and punch back when the time is right," he said.

"When all of this is over, we have to go away and get some Champ and Wanna time."

"I'm with that," Champ said, putting his hand on Wanna's leg.

When they got to the hospital, they parked in valet and went in to see what had happened to Rhonda. Sharon, Micky, and Toot were in the waiting area with sad looks on their faces.

"Hey boys...what's up, girl?" Wanna said, giving a slight wave to Micky and Toot while hugging Sharon.

"What's up, Aunt Wanna?" Micky said.

Toot just waved back.

"What's up, Sharon?" Champ said, as he reached in for a hug.

"What's up, Champ?"

"Yo, let me holler at y'all outside," Champ said, pointing at Micky and Toot as he walked out. They followed behind him.

"What's up, Micky...what happened?"

"Champ, we moved all the bulky and valuable shit out of the apartment and I had Rhonda go by the spot to pack up come of my good clothes because I had to take care of some business. When me and Toot got back about an hour and a half later, she was on the floor full of blood and her skirt was pulled up damn near over her face. Somebody raped my girl, Unc," Micky said, tears in his eyes.

"Did it look like a robbery gone bad or did it look like somebody just came to hurt Rhonda?" Champ asked.

"Unc, there wasn't nothing to take and the crib wasn't ransacked."

159

"Get your step-pop on the phone," Champ directed.

"I called him and he pushed the button to send me straight to voicemail then he turned his phone off," Micky told him.

"That's strange," Champ said, rubbing his chin.

"I said the same thing, and if I find out he had anything to do with this he's a dead man walking," Toot said, not giving a fuck about Tone being his family when it came to Micky.

"The only thing is that she knows Tone and she would have said his name to me if he was involved," Micky said.

"Well, when the doctor allows us to talk to her, we'll take it from there. Micky, I'm going to let the guns come out on this one," Champ said, not knowing Micky would bring them out regardless for Rhonda.

Chapter 15

Rhonda made out pretty well. She was more mentally and emotionally hurt than physically. She begged Micky and Sharon not to contact her parents. She didn't want her family to look at Micky in a different light. It wasn't his fault that someone was savage enough to break into his house and rape her. She knew he felt bad and she wouldn't allow anyone to make him feel worse. Not the doctors, police, her parents...nobody!

She loved Micky with her whole heart. The emotion he showed and the tears he cried when he discovered her body let her know in her heart that he loved her and confirmed that he was all the man she needed. She felt so comfortable when he held her and she felt safe from any harm when he was present. She never gave a description of her assailant to Micky because he wouldn't allow her to waste any of her energy trying to explain anything while she was slipping in and out of consciousness. He just wanted to get her to the hospital so she could get help. The doctors were very nice to her and the nurses loved her. Even through the bumps and bruises, you could see how adorable she was and she still had her pleasant character.

The doctor ran tests on her to see if she had any sexually transmitted diseases from the rape. Although the doctor said that there didn't seem to be any sign of forced penetration, it was procedure to check for STDs. She seemed to be clean but she wouldn't get a definite answer until her blood work came back, and even after that she would have to come back in six months to see if she had contracted H.I.V.

"Rhonda, girl, you'll be fine. I talked to the doctor and he said that the creep that raped you didn't seem to have penetrated you with his tiny dirty dick because there's no rawness or signs of abnormal stretching on your kitty-kat," said Rhonda's favorite Nurse Ericka, as she walked out and let Micky enter the room. Rhonda lit up as soon as she saw Micky come in.

"Hey, baby-girl, these are for you," Micky said, placing a vase arrangement of two and a half dozen Calla Lilies on the table next to her bed.

"Oh, my God, they are pretty. Thanks, baby," Rhonda said, smelling the flowers and avoiding eye contact with Micky.

Although she knew Micky was down with her no matter what, she was still embarrassed that she got raped and was self-conscious about her scars.

"Yo, look at me and listen, Rhonda. You didn't do anything wrong. I love you no matter what that bastard did. You're still as pure to me as you were the day I met you. I am your man and I'm here. Don't ever let me see you put your head down when you talk to me or anyone else. Talk and look at me with the same glow you always had, baby-girl," Micky said, holding Rhonda's face and looking directly into her eyes.

The nurse told Micky it was important to let Rhonda know she was not at fault.

"Micky, I should have heard that monster come in the door. I was so busy listening to the damn music that I didn't notice him until he was standing there with that damn gun," Rhonda said, now looking at Micky the way she used to.

"You didn't have no control over that. I should have been there," he said with regret.

"It's not your fault, Micky."

"Okay...I won't blame me if you don't blame me. Deal?"

"Deal," Rhonda said, squeezing Micky's hand.

"Rhonda, please tell me it wasn't Tone that did this," said Micky.

Rhonda was surprisingly confused by Micky's question.

"Oh, no, baby, it wasn't Tone. As much as I dislike him, it wasn't him. Why do you think Tone would do something like this?" she asked.

"Rhonda, it's a lot going on and Tone has been acting funny."

"It was this brown-skinned, short guy and he had a dead left eye," she said, describing her assailant.

"Did he have a tattoo on his hand?"

"Yeah...on his right hand. I can't remember what it was because I was more worried about the gun he had," she told him.

Micky got quiet. He knew then it was Sab who had put his hands, and possibly his dick, on Rhonda. And he knew Sab would never bust such a move without Tone's approval. All he could think of was murdering Sab.

"I'm going to kill both of those faggot-ass niggas," Micky said softly to himself.

"Huh?" Rhonda said, trying to hear what Micky was mumbling about.

"Oh, nothing, baby," Micky said, snapping back to the present situation.

"Micky, I just want to get home and get back to my life with you. Promise that you'll be around for me for life," Rhonda said.

"Rhonda, I'm here and I'm not going nowhere," he promised.

~~~~~

Sharon and Wanna walked into the room just as Micky finished talking.

"What's up, baby? How are you?" Wanna said, hugging Rhonda.

"I'm okay, Wanna."

"What's up, daughter in-law?" Sharon said, almost knocking Wanna over to get a hug from Rhonda.

"What's up, Mom?" Rhonda replied, as she hugged Sharon back.

"I guess I don't get no love today," Micky said, with his arms folded. Both Sharon and Wanna hugged Micky.

"You feel better now?" Sharon said, as the women released Micky from their dual hug.

"Yeah, I feel loved now," Micky said laughing.

"Where did you get these beautiful flowers from?" Wanna asked, as she smelled the arrangement.

"Micky brought them for me."

"Boy, I'm proud of the fact that you are man enough to have your woman's back," Wanna said to Micky.

"Aunt Wanna, I'm just trying to play my part."

They all talked for a few minutes before Micky said goodbye to Rhonda and Wanna. He promised to get with Rhonda later before he kissed them both on the cheek. He asked his mom if he could talk to her before he left. She followed him into the hallway.

"Mom, have you heard from Tone?"

"No Micky, I haven't heard from him all night. When I called his phone it went straight to voicemail," she told him. Micky tried to hold back his emotions in front of his mother.

"Mom, Tone's man raped my girl. If Tone calls you or shows up, I want you to call me. If you can't get me then call Champ."

"Do you think Tone hurt that girl or had anything to do with it?" Sharon asked.

"Mom, I don't know. I just want to ask Tone what's up with his man and where dude is at," Micky said, lying through his teeth. He knew damn well he wanted to put a bullet in Tone's head.

"Baby, be careful. If that bastard had anything to do with that girl getting hurt, I'll put him out of his misery myself," Sharon said, in earnest.

"Mom...I only messed with and defended Tone because he made you happy, but he crossed the line if he had anything to do with this," he said.

"Baby, I know...baby, I know," Sharon said, as she attempted to comfort her only child. Micky kissed her on the cheek and left to pick up Toot.

Toot went to his Aunt Bernadette's house to pick up on his family and the whereabouts of Tone. Micky went to the loft to meet Toot to find out what he heard.

"What's up, Toot?"

"It ain't shit, Micky-Mick," said Toot.

"Did you hear anything about Tone's punk-ass?" Micky asked him.

"Naw, everybody is saying the same thing. They say he's not answering the phone, and when I called it two or three times it went straight to voicemail," Toot told him.

"Yeah, my mom said the same thing," Micky said, sipping spring water.

"The nigga is bitching and we just want to talk to him."

"Naw, Toot...it's past wanting to talk to the nigga. Rhonda told me today that the nigga, Sab, was the one that came through the door and raped her."

"Oh shit, that's crazy. That pussy would have never made that move without Tone's approval."

"That's what I was thinking when she told me," Micky said, "She said it was a dead-eye nigga with a tattoo on his hand."

"Yeah, that's Sab's bitch-ass all day," Toot agreed.

"I know. I should have hit that no good pussy when I rocked Rocky. I had the A-R pointed at them but I let him and his man live on the strength of Tone. I'm not letting up on them fleas this time," Micky vowed.

"Well, fuck him and my cousin. I'm with you. I say we shoot Sab in his dead-ass eye and Tone in his dead-ass arm after we kill them faggot-ass niggas."

"I'm shooting Sab in his dirty little dick for pulling that stunt with Rhonda," Micky said.

"Micky, I'm with you. How is Rhonda anyway?"

"She's good. The doctor said he don't even think Sab got his dick in her because he couldn't see any signs of forced penetration or scarred tissue. They ran several tests just in case. She has a black eye and some swelling in her face but she's good."

"Damn, homie...I fucks with Rhonda. She's good for you and she's good to you."

"Toot, we're going over Jersey and sit on that faggot-ass Sab at his girl's house tonight and then we'll catch up with Tone's bitch-ass."

"Micky, I'm with you. I'm telling you now that I'm not playing getaway driver on this one. I'm busting my gun too," Toot said, meaning every word.

"Toot, we can both bust our guns on this one. I'm going to shoot that nigga 'til he catch on fire."

"Damn, I like that, my nigga...that must mean we are bring the A-K's out," Toot said.

"Yeah, my nigga...we're bringing the A-K's out," Micky agreed, with a wicked smile on his face.

~~~~~

Bingo was feeling a lot better now that he went to court. He found out the charges against him; possession with intent to deliver five or more kilos, conspiracy, money laundering, and related charges. Teddy, Nino, and Jay-baby were all charged with the same thing. Bingo's lawyer was aggressively trying to get him bail through the U.S. Attorney. The Judge agreed to hear a bail argument in two weeks.

He noticed that both Champ and Thelma were in the courtroom to show their support. Champ never ceased to amaze everyone. He was the best of the best. Bingo didn't know how he would repay Champ for extending his hand to him on this one but he was going to try his best to repay Champ in any way he could. He was also pleased to talk to Jay-baby. The U.S. Marshals wouldn't let them be in the same cell because of the separation game the government was playing. Despite that, Jay-baby hollered over from his cell to assure Bingo that he would rather die than cross him because Bingo had been too good to him.

When they got back from court, Bingo called Thelma to express his thanks and love for her. He never mentioned Champ's name on the phone but he told her to tell her folks he appreciated everything.

Bingo returned to his cell to discuss the day.

"Yo, Bingo, that fucking U.S. Attorney was sick when Fred Perri was digging in his ass," said Nino, when Bingo walked in.

"Yeah, he's a beast in that courtroom, Nino."

"Shit...our lawyers didn't even have to say anything," Teddy said, eating a Twix.

"How the fuck they going to try to get the judge to deny me bail. They said I'm a flight risk...I've never been arrested in my life," Bingo said, thinking of the government as a vicious entity.

"Yo, if it comes down to it, I'll claim the whole case and y'all can just make sure I'm good until I get there. It ain't no use all of us sitting in here," Nino said, showing his ignorance about the federal system.

"Nino, it ain't that easy, baby-boy...and if it was, I wouldn't let you throw your life away that easy. We are going to put up the best fight we can," Bingo said, letting Nino know they were in the shit together.

"It's your call, big homie, but if you want me to stay and y'all go, I'm all for it."

"It's not that easy. He told your goofy-ass that we're rumbling this together," Teddy said, laughing and mugging Nino in the head. Teddy and Nino had been through a lot together and it strengthened them.

"Yo, what's up with them fires and shit? If we were home, niggas wouldn't have burned down the pool hall or the tire shop. Especially not the tire shop, because that was our lounge," Nino said, thinking of how quickly things turned around in a matter of days.

"Yeah, they said that Dawud's memorial was burned down, too," Teddy pitched in.

"I know. What type of faggot shit is that?" Nino said.

"I think nut ass Tone did that shit. He's a jealous pussy and he's burned out. He is the bad apple out of all of our niggas. The crazy part is the nigga really got money. I know the nigga should at least have a couple million tucked away. The way he ran around with all the hatin' bullshit you would think he was a broke nigga," Bingo said, letting off a little steam.

"Man, I thought we killed that pussy when we popped his nut-ass sister, Nay," Nino said in a low tone, while looking out the cell door to be sure no one overheard.

"I wish it was that pussy instead of whoever Nay had in the car."

"Who was that in the car with Nay?" Nino asked, still looking out of the door.

"Who knows, it could have been anybody. Nay likes eating them dicks and she likes it in the ass all crazy. Me and Dawud partied the bitch one time and the bitch wore both of us out," Teddy said, now thinking of how good Nay's dick-sucks were.

"Damn, I miss my boy, Dawud, with his greedy ass. I'm still going to out that nigga, Tone, when I get there and, if he ever comes through here, I'm going to cut his dead-ass arm off and beat him with it," Nino said.

"I miss Dawud, too. It's fucked up that we'll miss his funeral," Bingo said, picking up the Cash is King novel, *C.E.O.*, that Shaahir gave him to read.

"Yeah, we're going to miss our boy's funeral," Teddy said, throwing punches at an invisible opponent.

They talked until recall time. Recall is when every man goes back to his assigned cell. Teddy and Nino were cellmates, so they went to their cell after they gave Bingo some dap. Bingo didn't have cellmate yet. He just had four walls, a walkman, and a book, so he turned on the Quiet Storm, opened the book and began to read *C.E.O.*

~~~~~

Thelma and Champ had been together all day since they left the house early in the morning. Thelma was thankful to have her cousin at a time like this. Champ really came through for her. She knew that without Champ she would have been busting her ass to get Fred Perri to defend her husband. She was also thankful he let her stay with him and Wanna.

Champ felt as though he was just doing his duty. He didn't want any praise, because he felt like he wasn't doing anything special.

"Cousin, you're my angel, and I know my life would have been down the drain without you," Thelma said, pulling into the empty parking space in front of McCormick and Schmick's Seafood Restaurant where they were meeting Sharon and Wanna.

"Thelma, your life would have been fine without me. My life would have been down the drain if I didn't have you as a crazy-ass cousin," Champ said, reversing the compliment Thelma had just given him. He didn't want her to think that she owed him anything.

"Cousin, you're not flipping it this time. You are my hero and you always save me no matter how deep my troubles are," Thelma said, knowing Champ so well and knowing that he would try to downplay the fact that he came through for her yet again.

"Cousin, we're family and I honestly know that if it were the other way around you would do whatever to make sure I'm good. I told you that before, so let's not go down this avenue again."

"Okay, Cousin, but…"

"But, nothing. Let's go up in here. I'm hungry as all outdoors," Champ said, walking into the restaurant.

"Cousin, you be walking fast as heck. You know I got these heels on," Thelma said, jogging to catch up with Champ.

When they entered the lobby, the receptionist told Champ his party was waiting for him upstairs in a rear booth. Champ and Thelma went up to find their table. As soon as Sharon spotted them, she flagged them over to where she was sitting with Wanna.

"What's up, ladies?" Champ said, as he hugged them both and kissed Wanna.

"What's up, Champ? You're really looking good. You don't seem to be aging at all, Sharon said, realizing Champ was the only one left from the original crew. Bingo was booked, Ern was dead, and Tone had one foot in the grave.

"Sharon, you haven't aged neither."

"That's enough flirting," Wanna cut in jokingly. She knew Sharon's loyalty to her and Champ's loyalty to Ern.

"Let me find out that's somebody's way of saying they missed me today," Champ smirked.

All the girls laughed.

"You got me. I'm busted," Wanna said, kissing Champ on the cheek.

"Order me a Patron and pineapple juice," Champ said, as he stood up.

"Where are you going?" Wanna asked.

"I'm going to the bathroom. I need that drink like yesterday because I had a long day," Champ said, walking off to the restroom.

"Girl, you got a winner there," Sharon said.

"Yeah, Wanna, my cousin is a hell of a dude," Thelma said, as the waiter walked over.

"May I help you, ladies?"

"Yeah, bring us out some crab cakes, three martinis and one Patron and pineapple," Wanna said. The waiter left to place the order.

"Girl, I know your cousin is one hell of a man and that's why I don't want him in them streets. I would die if something were to happen to him. I now know what the boy in *Brown Sugar* meant when he told the girl, 'you're my air'," Wanna said, taking a bite of her bread.

"To be honest, Wanna...Champ is all of our air. He's saved all of us one time or another," Sharon said, honestly.

Champ returned from the restroom and sat down next to Wanna.

"Sharon, what's up with Rhonda?"

"She's fine. The doctors said that, outside of the bumps and bruises, she's perfectly fine. Everything else is mental and emotional."

"I'm glad to hear that because shorty blends right in with this family."

Everybody agreed with Champ's statement.

"I can't believe someone would do something like that to that sweet girl," Thelma said, shaking her head.

"That was some coward shit and they say a coward dies a thousand deaths," Champ replied.

The waiter brought their drinks and appetizers. They ordered their main course and Champ told the waiter to bring them another round of drinks. They all had a good time laughing and joking with each other. They spent some time reminiscing on the days when life was better. All and all, it was a good night for everyone. They promised to get together like this at least once a month. Champ paid the bill and gave the waiter a nice tip. Sharon headed to Delaware while Thelma, Wanna, and Champ headed toward Champ's house.

Chapter 16

Weeks went by and there were no signs of Tone anywhere. He hadn't been past Sharon's house and he changed his phone number. He hadn't been seen in any of his usual spots. His mom was worried about not hearing from him and she was actually contemplating issuing a missing persons report on him.

Although he did a lot of fucked-up things and hurt a lot of people, Sharon didn't want anything bad to happen to him. She just wanted at least to talk to him to make sure he was okay. She also wanted to know if he had anything to do with Rhonda's assault. She needed to hear him say flat out that he had nothing to do with it. Sharon couldn't imagine Tone having anything to do with a rape. Her concern for him was genuine. Thoughts of Tone being either hurt or dead began to surface in her mind. He just disappeared without touching any of the money they had in the bank or what was in the floor safe. Sharon didn't know the combination to the safe, but she knew exactly where it was located and could tell that the safe hadn't been opened by the fact that the carpet wasn't torn or disturbed.

Sharon was waiting on Micky to come so they could go to the dealership in New Jersey to get his new car. She knew Micky could care less about what happened to Tone because of what he told her regarding Rhonda's incident.

Despite that, she was going to ask him if he had heard anything in the streets about Tone. While she was waiting on Micky, her phone rang and she picked up on the first ring. She had gotten in the habit of answering on the first ring, wishing it would be Tone.

"Hello."

"What's up, girl?" Wanna said, from the other end of the receiver.

"Nothing, girl...I'm just a wreck hoping this damn man is okay. I don't even look at the caller I.D. I just pick up on the first ring hoping his ass would just call and say he's okay. I hate the bastard but I don't want anything to happen to him," Sharon said, knowing damn well she didn't hate Tone.

She just said it to make Wanna think that she wasn't a sucker for Tone. Little did she know, Wanna was already hip to her. She knew Sharon loved Tone and she also knew how silly love could make a person. Wanna would never make Sharon feel like a nut for being a fool for Tone. She was going to remain a true friend to Sharon no matter what.

"Did you go on the state and federal prison system website to see if he's locked up?" Wanna asked, "Tone is okay. He's a survivor, so he'll always make sure he's okay," she finished, attempting to comfort Sharon but not really caring if Tone was in jail or dead.

"Girl, I did all of that and I came up with nothing."

"He'll pop up, Sharon," Wanna said, hoping that the nigga would pop up dead.

"Forget that, girl. What's up? What did you want?" Sharon asked.

"Me and Thelma were going to the mall and I was wondering if you wanted to go," Wanna said.

"I do, but I can't...I'm going to the car dealer with Micky," Sharon replied.

"Do you want me to get you something while I'm out?"

"No, I'm cool."

"Well, hit me when you and Micky get back from getting the car. Tell my nephew I said hi."

"Okay, girl, I'll call you later," Sharon said, hanging up.

She went to check the computer to see if there was an Anthony Davis as a new commit. Just like yesterday and the day before, she came up empty.

Sharon's focus on Tone was interrupted when Micky called to let her know he was outside. She gathered her things together and left out the house to get into the car.

"What's up, Mom?"

"Nothing, Son. What's up with you?" Sharon said, kissing Micky on the cheek.

"What's wrong, Mom?" Micky said, sensing stress in his mom.

"Micky, I know you think Tone played a part in what happened to that pretty girl of yours, but you're not sure."

"I'm not sure, Mom, but I hope he didn't," Micky responded, knowing that his mom was stressed out over Tone.

He didn't want her to sense that he was going to kill Tone when he came across him, no matter how long it would take for them to cross paths.

"Well, you know I love Rhonda like a daughter. If he had something to do with it, I'd hurt him myself just as fast as you would. I just want to be sure he really had something to do with it before I condemn him."

"Mom, I agree but we can't find him and no one seems to have his phone number."

"Damn, that's what I wanted to ask you. Did you hear anything on the streets on where he could be?" Sharon asked, with a hint of desperation in her voice.

"Mom, it's like he really disappeared. Toot said that Ms. Bernadette is considering putting a missing persons report out on him if he doesn't show up this week."

"Yeah, I talked to her last night and she informed me of that. I hope the fool is okay," Sharon said, thinking the worst.

"Mom, I really hope that Tone didn't play a part in Rhonda's rape. I don't think he would do that knowing that she's my girl," Micky said, to make his mom feel as though he wasn't looking for Tone.

Honestly, Micky wasn't interested in hurting Tone...he wanted to kill him. He spent his nights in Jersey with Toot. They rode around the spots where they used to meet Tone and Sab hoping they would run across them.

Last week they scoped out Sab's cousin's house for about three hours to see if Tone or Sab would show up. After the long wait, they finally saw Sab's cousin come out of the house with some smut chick. Toot walked up and hit Sab's cousin all up in the face with an A-K. The poor boy didn't stand a chance; he died on the spot. It was all over the news. Micky hoped that it would bring Tone and Sab out of hiding, or at least Sab so he could get at the nigga for Rhonda. Micky was beginning to believe Tone and Sab were somewhere dead or tied up because there was no way for them to just up and disappear.

"Mom, did you call up the jails to see if he was locked up?"

"I called the jails, Micky, and I even checked the websites."

"Federal and state?"

"Yes."

"He'll show up, Mom."

"I hope so."

They drove over to F.C. Kerbeck listening to the radio. Sharon was relieved that Micky was giving Tone the benefit of a doubt. She would still be thinking Micky wanted to hurt Tone if they had never had this conversation. Micky's thoughts were different, although he was happy that he was able to put his mom's mind at ease where Tone was concerned. The fact of the matter was that Micky had every intention of killing Tone and nothing could stop him...not Sharon, not the law, not anyone.

<center>~~~~~</center>

Champ was meeting Ducky at Champions. They normally didn't meet late in the day, but Champ got stuck in the crib with Wanna trying to get a quickie off while Thelma was out seeing Bingo. It'd been awhile since he could bang Wanna all around the house because Thelma had practically moved in. He decided to push back his meeting so he could take advantage of his girl.

When he pulled up, Ducky was already there. It never failed; Ducky always beat Champ to a meeting spot. Just like every other time, he waited in the car until Champ pulled up and they walked in together. They went straight back to their normal meeting booth.

"Damn, Ducky, you're gaining weight," Champ said playfully, while acknowledging the fact that Ducky has been turning it up on the streets lately.

In fact, Raheem, Ducky, Toot, and Micky were all doing more numbers and making more money in the last few weeks than they ever had before. It was in part because of Bingo being locked up and because Tone allowed his jealousy to crumple his empire. Champ's crew was the only crew left on the scene. Champ was fair with his crew, which in turn meant that they could be fair to the people who copped off them. Niggas were really starting to see how much better off the city was without Tone. There was a sudden stop in gunplay and things were peaceful.

"Yeah, it's been raining paper. When a nigga is making money he tends to eat better," Ducky said, rubbing his stomach.

"I hear that. What's been going on down the way? Has anybody seen Tone? I noticed that all the gunplay has slowed down," said Champ.

"Naw, but wherever he's at I hope he stays because he fucks the whole hood up. Niggas be bitching as if he's built like that. They be like, *don't tell Tone I copped* after they buy off me. I always say, 'Fuck Tone'."

"Damn, Sharon is worried about that piece of shit nigga because he up and disappeared like that," Champ said, snapping his fingers.

"She don't need to be with that maggot-ass nigga any way. It's still rock on the spot with that nigga for doing that crazy shit to Micky's girl. Right?" Ducky said, trying to confirm he still had Champ's blessing to take care of Tone when they crossed paths.

"Yeah, it's still rock on the spot. I think Sharon would have more closure knowing his whereabouts...even if he's dead."

"I was happy as a nigga in Onyx Monday night with a bankroll when you gave us the green light to rock that nut-ass nigga. I really be having dreams about what I'ma to do to him."

"Don't forget he's not our main focus. Our main focus is this paper, but keep your ears to the streets," advised Champ.

"What's up with Bingo and them?" Ducky asked.

"They're good. Thelma went to see Bingo this morning but I haven't seen her yet to see if he sent me any messages."

"That's cool. Tell Thelma crazy-ass to tell Teddy and them niggas I said what's up."

Their meeting was over and, since they didn't order anything, they just got up and left. Ducky rolled out to go down the bottom and Champ was about to meet Micky to see his new car.

Micky shouldn't have been long at the dealership because he paid for the car yesterday with a certified check for the balance after Micky's trade in. Since it was going in Sharon's name, they just needed her signature and proof of insurance.

"Hello," Micky said, after seeing Champ's name on the caller ID.

"What's up, nephew? Did you get your car?"

"Yeah, I'm taking mom to meet up with Aunt Wanna and then I'll be on my way to link up with you," Micky told him.

"Alright, call me," Champ said, as he stopped at a red light thinking how life has been so good to him.

Boom! Crunch!

Somebody hit the back of his car. Champ was okay and he was thankful that the man pulled over. Champ figured he wouldn't put a hardship on the man by filing a police report since he was kind enough to pull to the side. Champ parked, turned his car off, and got out to assess the damage.

"Are you okay, my man?" the man asked Champ.

"Yeah, I'm good. Are you and your pass...." Champ began.

He never got the chance to finish his sentence because Sab cracked him over the head with the butt of his .45 Rugger twice. Tone pulled up in the van and they dragged Champ inside.

"Make sure you keep your eye on that pussy because he punches hard as shit. I don't want him to try to play hero. If he even looks like he's getting up, crack him in his mother-fucking head and put him right back to sleep," Tone said to Sab.

"This nigga is out cold, but if he gets up I'm going to split his shit again," Sab said, taking the money out of Champs pocket and removing the watch from his wrist.

"What the fuck are you doing?" Tone said, looking into the rearview mirror.

"Nigga, I'm getting iced out and taking the bread this nigga got in his pocket. He won't need this money any more," Sab said, trying on Champs watch.

"You're right about that," Tone smirked.

They drove on for fifteen minutes and pulled up out in back of some row homes on Anchor Street off of Summerdale in the Northeast. Tone hit the automatic garage door opener and waited for the door to open before he pulled the van into the garage and closed the door. Together, they carried Champ's body through the corridor that led to the basement.

"This nigga is bleeding like a motherfucker," Sab said, as he helped drag Champ through the basement.

"Fuck 'im...let's put him in the chair," Tone said, putting Champ in the chair he had cemented to the floor in his basement. Tone had tortured plenty of niggas and bitches in this very chair. They sat Champ up in the chair. Tone handcuffed Champ's hands behind the chair as Sab shackled his feet so that Champ didn't stand a chance of escaping when he woke up.

"Mummy that nigga, too," Tone said, tossing Sab the duct tape.

Sab circled the tape around Champ's midsection as well to decrease his mobility.

"Yo, watch him while I go get our medicine and a bucket of ice water."

"Go ahead...I got this nigga," Sab said, smacking the shit out of Champ.

Tone ran upstairs and came back down with two eight-balls of powder and a bucket of water. He put the bucket down and passed Sab an eight-ball of coke. They both snorted their raw powder before Tone threw the water into Champ's face. Champ began to regain consciousness. He was a little confused but he was certain about several things immediately. He knew he was hurt bad, he needed help, and Tone was behind it all.

Despite the beard and weight he had put on, Champ could see the same grimy Tone he had known since childhood.

"Rise and shine, my nigga, Champ," Tone said, with a wicked laugh.

"Tone, what's up, man? I need a doctor. My head is aching and I got blood everywhere," Champ managed to say.

"Shut up, pussy, and listen to me because I'm only going to say this shit once before my man starts sticking you in your knee with a hot ice-pick. Nigga, I need you to tell me where that paper is at. I'm not talking about no peanuts but some real paper. Give me the keys to a house where there's somebody that can get to that paper. When we leave to go get the paper, we are going to duct tape your mouth so no one will hear you scream, my nigga. If you bullshit us, we'll kill you when we get back. The harder you make it for us to get the paper the longer we'll take to get back and the greater your chances are to bleed to death...so don't play no games," Tone told Champ.

"Damn, Tone, is this about some paper? Let me go and I'll get you all the paper you want," Champ said.

Smack!

"Wrong answer, motherfucker!" Tone said, smacking the shit out of Champ with his good arm, "It's not about some paper...it's about *your* paper," he concluded with emphasis.

"Tone, I got a black Range Rover parked on Brandywine Street in front of my mom's old house. You work the stash box just like the old ones that me, you, and Ern used to get put in up New York. The keys are in the ashtray. There's $750,000 in there. That's the most cash I have in one place. You know I tie my paper up in the bank," Champ said seriously, knowing he'd probably get killed if he bullshitted this nigga. At least this way he could buy some time and hope that all the good he did would allow a miracle to befall him because that's what it would take to get him out of this.

"Champ, I'm not playing with you, dawg. If I go down there and shit ain't how you said it is, all bets are off. I'm coming back to kill you and then I'm letting my nigga rape Thelma and Wanna before I kill them bitches," Tone said, and Champ could hear the sincerity in his voice.

After they taped Champ's mouth shut, Tone and Sab headed for the door.

"I wish Ern was here to tell you how I get down, son," Sab hollered, as he walked out the door.

Champ couldn't believe what was happening. He tried to think through his pain but his mind was a jumble of thoughts. He thought he heard the nigga that was with Tone basically admit to killing Ern. He considered Thelma and Wanna and how he would rather die before being the cause of harm to either of them. The thought of his two favorite ladies made him sure of one thing and that was that he would not lose this round.

~~~~~

Micky was calling around looking for Champ and it was getting late, too late for Champ not to be answering his phone. Everyone was calling around asking people if they had seen or heard from Champ. Nobody seemed to have heard anything. Wanna called the police, and when they answered, they said he had to be missing for 24 hours before he could be considered a missing person.

Ducky got a call that Champ's car was on Rising Sun Avenue right off Germantown Avenue. Ducky and Micky rode together in Micky's Maserati and Toot and Raheem followed in Ducky's Benz.

"Micky, I hope Champ is just somewhere getting some head or something."

"Me, too, Ducky but the nigga Champ don't operate like this. He would never not answer none of his phones for my nigga. Plus, I see bad bitches trying to get Unc's attention all the time but, since he got with Aunt Wanna, he don't be paying them chicks no mind."

"Yeah, Micky, you're right, but if he was locked up he would have called by now."

"Ducky, I don't know what's up but I know my Aunt Wanna, Thelma, and Mom are trippin'."

"I know, my nigga, better not be hurt or it's lights out in this nut-ass city."

"I'm with you, Ducky. Champ is like my pop."

They drove the rest of the way in silence listening to the *American Gangster* soundtrack, both hoping that everything was good with Champ.

~~~~~

"Damn, Tone, that nigga really gave us all this money," Sab said, amazed by his first ever look at three quarters of a million dollars in cash.

Tone had been fleaing Sab so much that Sab never had more than $50,000 cash at one time.

"Man, this shit is peanuts. We got to torture this nigga some more so he can give us more bread."

"Tone, you can talk your ass off but $750,000 is a lot of bread."

"Not when I know this nigga is sitting on a few million. I'm splitting that nigga's shit again as soon as we get in there so he'll know we're not joking with his punk ass."

"If you hit that nigga in the head again he's gonna die on the spot and we won't get no more money anyway. I say we kill him, dump his ass in a dumpster and break that bread down 50/50."

"You don't say shit because you're not the boss. What you say don't mean shit...this is my show. Besides, who said it's 50/50. If I feel like being nice I'll give you $150,000, but this job ain't complete," Tone said, hitting the garage door opener and pulling in before closing the door.

"You're right, Tone. I'm out of line. A hundred and fifty-thousand is more than enough to kill this nigga."

Champ heard them come in and all hope left him. He was in real bad shape. Tone walked up to him and pulled the tape off Champ's mouth. Champ was basically half dead and didn't even have enough energy to talk.

"That little paper was a good start and we appreciate it but I know you have a few million in cash. I got over a million in cash laying around and I barely hustle any more, so I can imagine what your paper is like," Tone said to Champ.

Champ tried to muster up the strength to speak but no words would come out.

"Oh...since he can't talk and he wants to act like he's dying, crack him in his mother-fucking head again," Tone told Sab.

Crack!

Sab smashed Tone in the face with the gun instead of Champ, knocking Tone's teeth out. Before Tone could react, Sab was pounding away at him. Tone was bleeding badly. Sab raised the gun and emptied all nine of his .45 bullets into Tone's face, head, and chest. He walked into the garage, got in the van, and sped off. He drove away feeling like he did Dave some justice since Dave got killed while they were doing a hit that Tone rushed him into. Sab was on top of the world. He was $750,000 richer and he didn't have to worry about Tone holding all the bodies they did over the years over his head. He didn't bother shooting Champ because he was sure that, by the time somebody found them in that basement, both Champ and Tone would be dead and stinking.

"Fuck Philly, I'm staying my rich ass in Jersey where I belong," Sab said, as he rode over the Ben Franklin Bridge headed home.

Chapter 17

Knock, knock, knock…

"Is anybody home? It's the Philadelphia Police Department," the officer said sternly, for the third time looking at his Lieutenant.

The lieutenant gave the order to kick in the door without hesitation. About thirty officers accompanied him into the house.

"Cover the upstairs. You, cover the downstairs and be careful, there were reported gun shots," the lieutenant said, as he ordered his officers about the house.

As soon as the cops reached the bottom of the basement steps, they called for the lieutenant to come down.

"We have one dead and this one right here is on his way out. He barely has a pulse," stated the cop who was the first to discover the bodies.

"Uncuff him. Call the paramedics and tell them they're clear to come down here."

The medics came and put Champ on a stretcher. They immediately started working on his injuries.

"This guy is in bad shape. He lost a lot of blood and his vital signs are very low," one medic said to the other.

"Hang in there, guy. Fight, guy! Fight! Find something in this world to fight for and fight!" the medic demanded, trying to heighten Champ's will to live.

The medics were doing all they could to help Champ as the drove him to the Hospital of the University of Penn.

~~~~~

Ducky and Micky were the first to get the news that Champ was in the hospital. They were in the car trying to make sense of why Champ would park his car and leave it there with all of his phones inside when Ducky's cousin Rodney called and told him that Champ came through the hospital on a stretcher, all fucked up. Rodney, along with half the bottom, worked at H.U.P.

Ducky damn near lost his mind when he heard the news. Micky called his mom, who was with Wanna and Thelma and gave them the news. Everybody headed down to the hospital. There was a lot of police activity, which was normal considering the circumstances. They found drugs, guns, a dead man, and another man on the verge of death. The police wanted to know who was who and what actually occurred. Champ was clearly abducted so he wasn't under arrest. However, if he pulled through, he would have to justify how he wound up in a house full of drugs, how he got tied up, and how the other man ended up dead on the floor.

Once Wanna and Thelma showed ID, the cop posted in the lobby allowed them to talk to the nurse.

"I'm the charge nurse, Ms. Smith. How are you two related to the patient?" the nurse said, as pleasantly as possible.

"I'm his cousin, Thelma Ware, and this is his fiancé, Tawanna Loften," Thelma told the nurse.

"As you can see, this is a security situation as well as a health issue. At this point, I will only answer questions for you, Ms. Ware, since it's obvious you are immediate family because you have the same last name as the patient. Since you have verified Ms. Loften as his fiancé, I'll answer questions for her as well."

"What condition is he in, Nurse Smith?" Wanna asked, anxious to know the chances of Champ's survival.

"He's in critical condition. He's lost a lot of blood and he's in ICU. The doctors are in with him now giving him an emergency blood transfusion. His vital signs are very low. That being said, I want to assure you that the doctor in charge of him is not only the best we have but the best neurologist in the country. If anyone can get him through his head injury, Doctor Twitch is the one," explained Nurse Smith.

"What are his chances?" Thelma said, crying.

"Oh, let's be optimistic. I've seen people in worse condition than Mr. Ware pull through. The medical team here will do our job...Mr. Ware has to do his job by fighting to stay with us. It's also up to you two and your family and friends to pray to whatever God you believe in."

Although the nurse was trying to encourage optimism, Wanna broke down into tears at hearing Champ's condition.

"When will we be able to see him?" she asked.

"Once we stabilize him and clean up the nasty cut on his head, he should be ready to see you."

"Thanks, Nurse Smith," Wanna said, as she grabbed onto Thelma for a hug.

"No problem, ladies. I'll be here with him more than anyone on this staff. I'm in charge of his file, so when all's said and done we will be like family."

"We will be here all day, every day...at least one of us ...until it's time to bring Champ home," Wanna said, still hugging Thelma.

~~~~~

"Yo, the news is on," Nino said, letting Teddy and Bingo know so they could watch. They all sat at the table with Shaahir. The dayroom was quiet as Walt Hunter began his report.

This is Channel 3 Eyewitness New, and this is Walt Hunter live, on the 1200 block of Anchor Street in the Northeast at the scene of what appears to be a kidnapping gone wrong. The house behind me is where Police were called after neighbors reportedly heard gunshots earlier today. Sources close to the investigation said that when police entered the residence they discovered the lifeless body of Anthony "Tone" Davis in the basement. He had been shot several times in the face, head, and chest with a large caliber firearm by an unknown person who is believed to be Davis' accomplice in the alleged kidnapping of Philadelphia's ex-boxer and entrepreneur Charles "Champion" Ware, who was found barely alive.

"Reportedly, Mr. Ware was found duct-taped, handcuffed, and shackled to an iron chair, which was cemented to the floor of the basement in the home behind me. He has been listed in very critical condition as a result of a head trauma and tremendous loss of blood. The family has asked that everyone pray for the safekeeping of the victim and justice for the perpetrator of this crime. This investigation is still underway. We will deliver more details on this story as the investigation unfolds. I'm Walt Hunter and this has been an Eyewitness News live report."

Shaahir's grief was evident by the tears rolling down his face. The whole FDC knew that, although his gangster was tamed by the Islam practiced in his speech and action, Shaahir could turn back to Shiz at the drop of a dime. Shiz was his name before he became Muslim and Shiz was someone that all the niggas who ever crossed him were glad to see put to rest. They preferred the humble Muslim brother, Shaahir, who Shiz had become.

"Bingo, let me holler at y'all," Shaahir said, pointing at Bingo, Teddy, and Nino.

They all followed Shaahir to his cell where he turned on the water in the sink to full blast to muffle their conversation just in case somebody in the next cell was trying to ear-hustle them.

"Yo, they hurt my man. They hurt Champ. *Wallahi* (I swear by Allah), if my man don't pull through I'm hurting everything in the Davis family," Shaahir said, with venom in his voice and his eyes.

"We should have been rocked that nigga, Tone," Teddy said.

"What's the data on that nigga, Tone?" Shaahir said, speaking to no one in particular.

"He's a nut. I always told Champ he was jealous of him and to watch out for that nigga," Nino offered.

"Who is his squad and who do you think was in on this shit with him?" Shaahir said, full of questions.

"The nigga's favorite two homies were Bam and Rocky and he's the cause of both of them being dead. At least that's what the streets say," Bingo pitched in, not knowing about Sab.

"I don't have no more minutes left on the phone, so I need you to tell your wife to tell Ducky to come up here for tomorrow's visit."

193

Shaahir always communicated with Champ through Ducky. Champ would never talk business on the phone nor would he come into any prison. He did, however, put Ducky on Shaahir's list to keep a direct line of communication open in case Shaahir needed to get a message to Champ.

"I'll go do that right now," Bingo said, and left to call Thelma.

Shaahir talked to Nino and Teddy until Bingo got back. They had been kicking it with him every day since they'd been in jail. They knew Champ had a tight relationship with him, but they never realized how deep it actually was. Shaahir knew stuff about Champ that they didn't know.

They also knew the two were close because of Thelma's reaction towards him. If she saw Shaahir in the visiting room, she would hug him and kiss his cheek. Thelma was firm with Bingo when she let him know that there was never any funny business and that she wasn't disrespecting him. She insisted that Shaahir was like family. Bingo was cool with her kicking it with Shaahir because he was secure with his position with his wife and he saw that it was genuine, so he wasn't tripping.

"She said Ducky will be here first thing in the morning," Bingo reported, as he returned to the cell.

"Good looking, Bingo. What she say about my man? Is he doing better?"

"She said that everything is the same. His condition has neither progressed nor regressed but she's hopeful that he'll pull through. I've known him since childhood and he's always come out on top. You heard it here first...Champ won't let Tone get out on him like this. Champ will not lose," Bingo said, confident that his homeboy would pull through as he had on many other occasions.

"Damn, I hope he does. I'm about to offer *Salat* (prayer), and when I'm finish I'll be down your cell to finish kicking it," Shaahir said, as he began to wash for prayer.

~~~~~

Sharon was in disbelief that Tone would pull some crazy shit like this and get killed in the process. She told Ms. Bernadette that she wasn't coming to grieve with the family nor would she be involved in any funeral arrangements. Ms. Bernadette was mad but Sharon didn't give a fuck. Tone made his bed and, as far as Sharon was concerned, the piece of shit could just lie in it. Tone had made her life hell and she refused to get down on herself. She decided that she wasn't going to stress out over him and his bad blood.

When she saw Micky and Toot come back into the hospital with Rhonda she hurried over to them. The hospital was still chaotic with people coming and going, so she wanted to be sure that she talked to them out of earshot of anyone else.

"Son, how are you?" she asked Micky.

"Mom, I'm not going to lie... if Uncle Champ don't make it I don't know what I'm going to do," he told her.

"Me, neither," Toot said, before Sharon could say anything.

"Champ will be okay. Why do you think we all started calling him Champ? He's always been a winner," Sharon said, looking at Micky and then Toot.

"My cousin was a nut. I'm not even going to his funeral," Toot said, expecting Sharon to be upset. But, to his surprise, she said nothing in answer to his comment.

"Come here, daughter," Sharon said to Rhonda.

"I can't believe none of this stuff, Mom. Champ...of all people? I don't know what happened but, whatever it was, I know Tone could have worked it out with Champ," Rhonda said, as she embraced Sharon.

"Mom, Rhonda didn't want to stay in the house by herself so she wanted me to bring her over here. Toot and I have to go take care of a few things, so I'll be back later," Micky said, as he gave Rhonda a hug and kiss. Toot and Micky rolled out to meet up with Ducky and Raheem.

Rhonda and Sharon went to the food cart to get some coffee. When they returned to the waiting area, Thelma and Wanna were talking to the nurse. They waited until Wanna and Thelma were finished talking before they approached them. You could see pain written all over their faces. It had been a long day and they couldn't wait until it came to an end. They only left to change clothes and then come right back. It would be like that until their "Champion" returned.

"Hey, doll baby, come give me a hug," Wanna said to Rhonda.

"Aunt Wanna, are you okay?" Rhonda asked, hugging Wanna, whom she had come to love like a real aunt.

"I'm okay, baby. I just got to hold on. Baby, my whole world is riding on this one," she said.

"You better come give me my hug, too," Thelma said, grabbing Rhonda from Wanna like she was a stuffed toy animal.

"What's up, Cousin?" Rhonda said, hugging Thelma back.

"Nothing, I thought you didn't love your cousin no more because you're letting Wanna get all the attention," Thelma said jokingly.

Rhonda was really accepted and loved among these women and she loved it.

"Now, nobody is loving the ex-girlfriend of the rotten bastard that's responsible for all of our grief. I say all of our grief because Champ is the closest thing I ever had to a brother. In honor of Champ...I'm not even going to that bastard Tone's funeral," Sharon said, as she broke into tears.

"Sharon, I know you love Champ and I know you didn't have any control over that bastard's actions. If Champ doesn't pull through, I'll go to hell and whip Tone's one-arm ass myself," Thelma said, sipping the coffee Sharon had passed her.

"Thelma, Champ will pull through. He didn't come this far to lose to a sucker like Tone," Sharon said, while Wanna wiped her tears.

"Girl, we know where your heart is at and Champ knows as well. You're my sister," Wanna said, as she continued to wipe the tears that were streaming down Sharon's face.

"What did the doctor say about him?" Rhonda asked, changing the subject and the mood.

"That wasn't a doctor. That was the charge nurse, Ms. Smith, and she's an angel. She's been with Champ every step of the way. She's been super nice to us and has answered the two million plus questions that Thelma and I asked her. She said that the blood transfusion brought his vital signs up and they think they'll be able to move him from critical to stable by morning. She said that he's looking better and better by the hour. He's not all the way out the woods yet but, if he keeps fighting, we'll have him back in no time," Wanna said, with a sense of hope in her voice.

"Damn, that's the best news I heard in the last two days," Sharon said, as she took a sip of coffee.

"When cousin gets out of this mess, he's taking me to the mall for a week straight because tomorrow's my birthday and he's up in some damn hospital," Thelma said, being her naturally crazy self. All the women laughed knowing that Thelma was just being Thelma.

"If he pulls through, Thelma, I'll be so happy that I'll take you to the mall for a week straight on me," Wanna said, dead serious.

"Okay, I'm holding you to that."

They all sat together hoping Champ would pull through, no matter what the cost.

~~~~~

Micky and Toot were on their way to meet Ducky and Raheem so they could try to put all this shit together and devise a trap for Sab. There was no doubt in Micky's mind that Sab was there when all this bullshit went down. Micky couldn't believe that Tone had the heart to put his hands on Champ. Tone had crossed a lot of lines in the past, but this was by far the most shocking. Micky couldn't figure it all out and was tired of trying to make sense of it.

"Toot...how the fuck did they get Champ out of the car without a struggle?"

"I don't know, Micky. I was over here thinking about that myself. That nigga, Tone, is a crafty piece of shit.

The only people at his funeral will be Aunt Bernadette and Nay," Toot said, knowing that there would be a little more than that, but certain he wouldn't attend.

"That nigga got off the hook easy. He was supposed to die of torture. He is a piece of shit. When we catch up with Sab we got to hit this nigga crazy," Micky said.

"Micky, I'm with you until the end. I don't have that nigga's bad blood up in me. We're related on my father's side anyway. Fuck Tone and Sab's dead-eyed ass."

"Toot, I know you're with me and I don't second-guess you, homie," Micky said, pulling up in front of Ducky's crib and calling his phone so he'd let them in.

Raheem came to let them in about two minutes after Ducky answered.

"What's up, little niggas?" Raheem asked, giving both men some dap.

"Ain't shit...we just chilling," Toot responded for the both of them.

"Yeah, we're chilling," Micky confirmed.

Ducky came downstairs and greeted everyone before he took the floor.

"Yo...niggas done hurt big homie and that's a no-no. We're going to handle this and we're going to handle it fast. Unfortunately, Tone's bitch-ass died before one of us could kill him. I swear if I could wake this maggot up and kill him again I would. We need to find out who else was there with Tone when he grabbed big homie. There's no way he could have done this alone if he had two arms, let alone this nigga only had one. Anyway, when we were in Onyx, big homie said this is the family so I got to ride with who's in this room. We don't want no outside help because this shit is personal," Ducky said, as he turned to look at Micky and Toot, "Do y'all know anybody else who could have had their hands in on this shit?" he asked the two.

"Yeah, his man, Sab, from over Jersey. That's supposed to be Tone's gun, but all of his shit that I've seen is amateur shit. I want to get the nigga myself because that's the nigga that raped my girl," Micky said, wanting Sab bad as a motherfucker.

"You can't get him by yourself. That faggot got to be target practice. We're going to air that nigga together," Ducky said, happy to discover the culprit.

"Ducky, I'm going to play team ball but, once this faggot drops or we grab him, however it goes, I need my face to be the last thing he sees before he checks out," Micky stated.

"Micky, we can do that for you," Ducky agreed. "We just have to find the nigga first."

"The nigga used to beat this little bitch house that live on Division Street off Haddon Avenue in Camden, but he hasn't been there. We've been laying on that spot since the nigga did that sucka shit to my girl. He also used to stay at his cousin's house over there, but I heard that nigga got rocked last night when he was leaving out," Micky said, with a wicked grin.

"Well, let's go lay over the bitch's house on Division Street and see if the little birdie pops-up," Ducky said, more or less telling them rather than asking.

"Let's go...we're out. Y'all can follow me and Toot. We got that Chopper and that Cal Tech that shoot 40 bullets all crazy."

They left and headed over the bridge with one common goal and that was to murder Sab. All four of them wouldn't feel like they did right by the man who looked out for them and made them comfortable unless they killed that one-eyed bastard, Sab.

Chapter 18

Sab had a new life. He was his own boss and even had a new nickname. He started having all the little hustlers in his new hood call him Apache. He wore a patch over his dead eye. He still snorted coke here and there, but he wasn't strung out like he was when he was rolling with Tone. The nigga had turned it up a few notches on the hustling tip. The $750,000 combined with the money and coke that he doubled back and took out of another one of Tone's stash houses was more than enough cushion to get the worse hustler on top.

He was buying work from some Spanish dude named Rick from up New York that he met through Tone a few years back. The fact that he didn't come with his hand out was a plus for Rick, too. He could move his product and not have to worry about what happens to it when it was gone. The more Sab bought, the more Rick dropped the prices. Sab was flooding Willingboro with coke for a cheaper price than the hustler's had ever seen. Because of the sudden drop in prices and the better quality of coke, Willingboro turned into a gold mine. The hustler's there used to have to take a fifteen-minute drive to Camden to cop their coke and then take the risk of driving it back. Sab was the answer to their hustling dreams. Everybody was trying to cop off Apache. He was no longer the little, dusty, gun-totin' Sab from Camden. He was now the big-body, Benz driving, VVS diamond wearing, big bankroll, got-it-for-cheap Apache from Willingboro.

The hustlers from Willingboro brought Apache's name up every time niggas from different cities brought up their top ballers. They would say how Apache came through driving this or that, how sick his jewels were, or things like how he bought the bar out at events. He was their guy. He couldn't believe how quickly he was running this town.

Initially, he came to hide out over his chick, Keisha's, house. He ended up getting her brother to middle-man the work he took from Tone's crib to the hustler's out there. Her brother moved the coke fast, brought every dime back, and was begging for more. So Sab went and copped a few pieces from up New York, gave them to her brother, and that shit moved just as fast. With such a quick, safe and profitable flip, Sab decided he wasn't going anywhere. With his new hood and his new name, he felt like a new man. He knew the only one who could change that was Champ.

He kept tabs on Champ's condition through the newspaper and the news. He began to regret leaving Champ behind without putting a bullet in his head. He was sure Champ wasn't snitching on him because, in all the interviews, Champ's lawyer firmly stated that Champ was unaware of the identity of the second abductor because he wore a mask. Today's paper made him nervous because it reported that Champ was being released from the hospital after making a full recovery.

"I know the nigga didn't snitch, yet but I don't know what this nigga will do under pressure. I should have killed that bug-ass nigga. The newspaper got this nigga on goody-two-shoes status. This punk-ass nigga sells just as much coke as anybody else, so why are they praising him?" Sab said aloud to himself, "I got too much going on right now to let this nigga come along and fuck this up. I'm going over Philly tonight and do some homework on that nigga so I can put dirt on him. He won't fuck up this Apache life I'm living," he concluded, while stopped at a red light at Levitt Parkway.

Just as he was about to get back to business, a van tapped the back of his Benz. It wasn't a bad hit. It was just a little bump. Sab had too much going on to sweat a little fender bender but his petty ways made him sweat the small stuff. He pulled to the side and approached the man that had exited his van wearing a pinstriped suit.

"What the fuck...this church-suit wearing asshole driving this busted-ass van can't see where he's going?" Sab said to himself, as he approached the man who seemed to be a little shaken.

"I'm sorry, sir. I guess my foot let up off the break while I was talking on my cell phone. I'm sorry I hit your expensive car but I'm thankful there's no damage," the man said, gesturing toward Sab's car so he could see there was no damage to the bumper.

After Sab turned to see there was nothing wrong with his car, he decided to scare the man who was already shaking.

"Watch the fuck where you going, you punk motherfucker. That's a $90,000 car. Do you understand?" Sab said, sternly.

"Sure...I understand and I don't want no trouble, sir."

"Just watch your fucking self," Sab said, walking away.

Before he could get back into his car, Ducky cracked him on the head with his gun. He hit him about three times before Raheem pulled up in the van. They threw Sab's body into the van and pulled off. Micky and Toot were following them just in case they couldn't grab the nigga on the same bump-and-run shit that Sab and Tone pulled off on Champ. They were unsure of whether or not they would get Sab with the old hit-on-the-bumper trick to lure him out of the car, but they did. Now they would be able to torture the nigga instead of shooting him and giving him an easy death like Tone.

They drove to Champ's warehouse on Delaware Avenue. Once inside, they dragged Sab to the back of the warehouse and handcuffed him to a cement mixer. It took every bit of patience Micky had in his body not to shoot Sab in the face and end it all. It was already understood that this was Micky's show. The whole crew knew it was personal.

Smack...Smack...Smack!

Get your dead-eye ass up, pussy," Micky yelled at Sab.

"Ha-ha...it's little Micky Mouse," Sab said, laughing when he came through and realized Micky was running the show.

"Little Micky, my ass. Pussy, you put your hands on my girl."

"Naw...I put this dick on your girl until your save-a-hoe-ass step-pop came through and saved the pretty little bitch. Micky ... that's a bad bitch," Sab said, with one hand cuffed to one mixer on his right and the other cuffed to one on the left. His ankles were tied together as well, which further limited his movements.

Micky walked up to him and stabbed him in the nuts with a hot soldering iron that he had kept plugged in since the morning.

"You faggot-ass nigga," he said as he held the iron.

Sab let out a cry of pain so agonizing that none of them had ever heard the likes of it before. You could smell the flesh and burnt hair. Micky pulled the iron away from Sab.

"Damn, nigga, it looks like your rape game will never be the same," he said, in mock pity.

Sab couldn't do anything but wheeze and cry. Toot took a screwdriver and stabbed Sab in each foot.

"Jesus walks, my nigga," he said, as he drove the tool into Sab's feet.

Sab started to fade in and out of consciousness. The shit was getting messy and heart-rending to these cold-hearted niggas. Ducky pulled out his burner but, before he could shoot, Sab started laughing and talking crazy as a result of the shock.

"I killed Ern...I killed Ern for Tone. Micky, I took your punk-ass in the hallway with your little Spiderman draws. Do you remember? Huh, pussy...do you remember me?" Sab taunted with a wicked smirk on his face.

"Pussy, what you say?" Micky said, knowing that Sab knew a detail that only someone present the night his dad died would know.

"Ha-ha...you heard me. You had them tight-ass Spiderman draws on. Now, kill me, nigga...kill me," Sab said, as he began shaking from the pain.

Micky snatched the gun out of Ducky's hand and shot Sab in the face, emptying the whole clip. He wished he could do the same thing to Tone. He was crying tears of hate. Hate for the men who took his world from him. Micky became a new man at that very moment. His understanding of 'trust no one' in this messy game he chose to be in was now a reality. He couldn't believe that his dad's friend fucked up his life.

Something snapped in Micky and he began beating Sab's lifeless body. Ducky had to actually pry Micky's hand off the gun and walk him away from Sab's body. Raheem and Toot cleaned up Sab's remains and wrapped him in hazardous waste bags so they could throw him in a dumpster. There wasn't a clue to the murder of Camden's Sab or Willingboro's Apache. The events of that incident were muffled by the sounds of heavy machinery and the silencer on the gun.

~~~~~

Ducky and Raheem were going to get at the nigga, Robby, who was supposed to testify against Bingo and them in their federal case but, by the time they got to his spot, the cops were everywhere. When they got to the hideout, they learned from the news that somebody had shot the nigga.

"Damn, my nigga, somebody handled that shit already."

"Yeah, fuck it. As long as the nigga, Robby, can't come to court Bingo should be cool," Ducky stated, as he dialed Micky's number.

"This nigga must be with his girl because he has his phone turned off," Raheem speculated.

"So, maybe that wasn't his Park Avenue we seen leaving Robby's block."

"I don't know, Raheem, and I don't care. I was just calling to make sure he's good."

"That nigga surprised me, how he put that work in on Tone's man," Raheem said.

"Yeah, Raheem, it looked like he turned into the devil in that fucking warehouse."

"That nigga, Tone, was a piece of shit. I always told Champ about that nigga," Ducky said, hating that Tone not only killed Ern and kidnapped Champ but betrayed Micky and had him around the nigga that killed his pop.

"Yo, what's crazy is all the money we spent on the streets trying to get up with this Sab nigga from Camden and Shaahir call me up to the jail and give me all the data about the nigga being in Willingboro under a new name. We might have to go take over that Willingboro shit one day. It ain't no use in letting a good town go to waste," Ducky mused.

"Ducky, that shit was crazy. How we caught up to the nigga and he was wearing that patch over his eye calling himself Apache," Raheem said.

"How about fuck him and fuck Tone. I'll murder them niggas ten times over for Champ and Ern," Ducky said, calling Micky's phone again.

Chapter 19

Champ was feeling like his old self again. He bounced back from near death and was now feeling more alive than ever. He counted his blessings and valued the ones that stuck with him through his hardship. In fact, he appreciated the hardship more now that it had come and gone. It allowed him to see who was who. Just like with anyone else who suffers a hardship and leaves money on the street, from imprisonment, hospitalization, or death, most of the people who owe you paper keep it moving. A few people handed the money owed to Champ over to Ducky and the rest of them caught what the streets called Hustler's Amnesia. Champ didn't sweat the small stuff; although one way or another, he got what was owed him.

Ducky, Raheem, Toot, and Micky were his street family. Sharon, Thelma, Rhonda and Wanna were his in-house family. These were the people who'd been tested and they all passed by being so supportive and loyal throughout his ordeal. Champ held them all very close to his heart. Although Thelma was still staying at the house with him and Wanna, Champ and Wanna did a lot of making up for lost time when he returned home.

Tonight was Champ's appreciation dinner. He was looking forward to seeing all of his loved ones in one room. Thelma was up in her room getting dressed with her music on, so it was easy for Champ to get a quickie off with Wanna. As of late, all he could get was a quickie. He would never ask Thelma to leave but he couldn't wait until Bingo got out so he could enjoy fucking Wanna's sexy ass all over the house again.

"Come on...let me lick that pussy like a stamp real quick," Champ said, smiling at Wanna who was only wearing a t-shirt.

"Damn, you are nasty, but I love it," Wanna said, kissing Champ on the lips.

He kissed his girl back and put his tongue in her mouth. He never got a chance to lick her pussy. She was so turned on and didn't want Thelma to come knocking before she reached her climax so she straddled on top of his already hard dick. He initially dicked her down long and slow but then he grabbed her waist, picked her up, and pulled her down harder and harder until they both exploded.

"You're nasty, girl."

"Shit, a sister got to get hers whenever she can. Orgasms are hard to come by as of late," Wanna said, laughing but serious.

"Don't worry, boo, Bingo starts trial next week. It's a good chance he'll win, so Cousin will be going home with her husband soon," Champ said, knowing that Wanna loved Thelma but was used to it being just the two of them around the house.

She had become accustomed to being fucked in the bedroom but truly missed being bent over sinks, washers, counters, couches, and whatever else they came across while in the mood. She loved being fucked all over the house by the love of her life, but they had to tone it down and be modest while Thelma was there.

"Baby, I'm not sweating Thelma being here. I actually like her being around," Wanna lied, only to make sure her man didn't feel guilty. They jumped in the shower and got ready to meet up with everyone for dinner.

~~~~~

Trev was originally from Philly but he moved to Atlanta, Georgia, in 2000. He didn't like Philly any more after he relocated. He learned how to hustle in Philly, but didn't really get his break until he moved down to Atlanta. He turned it up and was really getting at a dollar down there. He visited Philly every so often but this time he was coming for Tone's funeral. He had intentions of coming to the funeral and flying right back out until Nay told him a bunch of foul shit that made him stick around a little longer. He wasn't a cold-blooded killer but he had killed before.

He grew up in the same house as Tone, so they were close like brothers. Nay had been pulling his emotional strings knowing he was fucked up about Tone's death. He pulled up to Ms. Bernadette's house and Nay came out and jumped into the car.

"What's up, Trev?" she asked.

"Nothing, Nay, I'm chilling," he answered.

"When are you going back to Atlanta?"

"After I see what's up with this bitch, Sharon. She ain't just going to get out on my folks like that. I know she got Tone's paper and her stinking ass didn't even come to the funeral," Trev said, irritably.

"I know, Trev. She ain't shit and Toot's corny ass is all up her son's ass because he got a little Maserati. Corny-ass niggas," Nay said, hating as always.

"I'm not feeling Toot's bitch-ass neither. How the fuck he gonna miss his own cousin's funeral?" Trev said, trying to get a grip on the situation.

"Toot was a Tone hater just like everybody else in this city. They were all mad because Tone ran this city," Nay said, not even convincing herself of that shit.

"Let me get the keys to your apartment since your staying with your mom. When I'm about to leave town, I'll put the keys and some money in the mailbox," Trev promised.

Nay passed Trev her keys and was out.

~~~~~

Everybody was excited about the return of Champ. Even the haters had to love it. Ducky, Raheem, Toot, and Micky were all doing better than ever. They were a reflection of their main man and they all rolled with that in mind. Everybody pulled his own weight and moved as a unit. There was no room for the Tones of the world to come around and fuck up what they had going on.

With that in mind, they began to live by their new slogan, *There's no room for new friends...If we don't know you, we won't know you.*

The bad blood was gone the minute they put Tone in the ground. Tonight's dinner wasn't about Champ, but about his four guys and four girls. They all arrived at the Charter House restaurant on Columbus Boulevard on time for their reservation. Champ had the back of the deck reserved. There was a genuine feeling in the air among the party of nine. The waiter brought their drinks and appetizers along with several bottles of champagne.

Throughout the night, each person had their one-on-one time with Champ. He was happy to be among his people. These people could be locked in a dungeon with Champ and he would be just as happy there as he was in this restaurant at this moment. These were the people he loved.

After they ate, they had a champagne toast headed by none other than Champ.

"When I didn't know where I was going to get the strength from to get out of that bed, or if I was ever going to get out, each and every one of you gave me the strength I needed to get up and get back," he said, toasting all of them at once. He then turned to look at each person as he addressed what they provided him. He continued with his tribute.

"Everyone helped: from the pity in the eyes of Rhonda; the pleading of *Champ, pull through* from Sharon; the *Unc, I can't lose you like I lost my dad from Micky*; the look of *if you don't get up, I'm going to murder everybody in the city* on Raheem and Ducky's faces; to the *Cousin, I need you to get up so I can get you to take me to the mall* look on Thelma's face; or the *big homie, I need your guidance* look on Toot's face."

He turned to Wanna and gazed into her eyes.

"Last, but not least, the *get up, we've got some unfinished business and I'm supposed to be your wife* look on Wanna's face."

Wanna leaned in and kissed Champ before allowing him to finish. He looked back to the group of people that he considered to be his beloved family.

"All y'all combined gave me the strength to be here with y'all and I love each and every one of you for his and her personal essences. Here's to us!" Champ said, holding his glass in the air.

Everybody drank their champagne to toast the words of their champion. The night was a smash. Everyone was happy to be a part of this celebration of life with Champ.

At the end of the night, everybody got into his or her car and headed home. Sharon was emotionally stuck between two worlds. She was happy for Champ, he was like the brother she never had. On the other hand, she was afraid to let him or any of the others know that she had bad blood growing inside of her. With all the morning sickness and new cravings, she decided to go to the doctor's to get a pregnancy test. She found out that she was pregnant with Tone's baby and, although she hated Tone for what he did to her life, she was leaning toward keeping the baby. With her mind clouded by thoughts of what to do about the baby, she never noticed the black, tinted-out Benz that was following her down 95 South. It had followed her to the restaurant and now it was following her home.

Breinigsville, PA USA
01 March 2010

383BV00001B/2/P